Book Two of the Yesterday Series

A Novel By

Amanda Tru

Published by

Sign of the Whale Books™

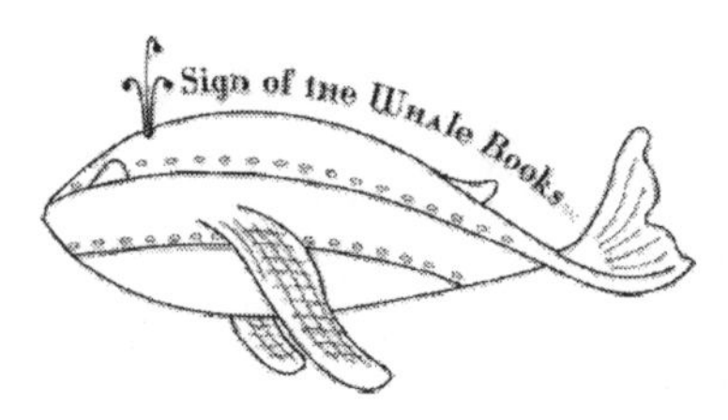

Copyright Notice

The Locket
Book 2 of the Yesterday Series

PUBLISHED BY: *Sign of the Whale Books*™*, an imprint of *Olivia Kimbrell Press*™, P.O. Box 4393, Winchester, KY 40392-4393. The *Sign of the Whale Books*™ colophon and Icthus/spaceship/whale logo are trademarks of *Olivia Kimbrell Press*™.
**Sign of the Whale Books™ is an imprint specializing in Biblical and/or Christian fiction primarily with fantasy, magical, speculative fiction, futuristic, science fiction, and/or other supernatural themes.*

Cover Art and Graphics by Debi Warford (www.debiwarford.com)

Library Cataloging Data

Tru, Amanda (Amanda Tru) 1978-
The Locket, book 2 in the Yesterday Series/Amanda Tru
250 p. 20.32cm x 12.7cm (8in x 5in.)

Summary: Time traveling to solve the mystery could cost all the time she has left.

ISBN: 978-1-939603-73-9

1. time travel 2. christian romantic mystery 3. new adult 4. male and female relationships 5. parodoxes

[PS3568.AW475 M439 2012]
248.8'43 — dc211

The Locket

Book Two of the Yesterday Series

A Novel By

Amanda Tru

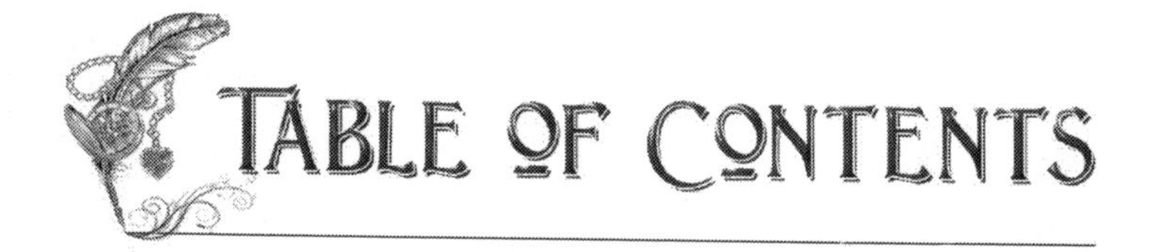

Table of Contents

CHAPTER ONE

I immediately started trembling from head to toe. This could not be happening! Not again!

Just two minutes ago I'd been stealing a few minutes in Seth's arms. He'd told me he loved me. We'd been on our way to pick up my medical records from the offices in the Jackson hospital. We walked down the hall and now faced a solid wall that shouldn't be there.

I closed my eyes, trying to breathe deeply. The decor was wrong, the layout was wrong, everything about the hospital wasn't as I clearly remembered.

And I knew. This had happened before.

Seth didn't know. Not yet. It's not like my boyfriend had ever experienced this with me before. But this was the third time in my life I'd turned around to find everything different from mere seconds before.

There was only one explanation. I had time traveled again.

But there was one change this time. I opened my eyes and looked at Seth. This was the first time someone else was experiencing the same thing I was.

I needed to tell him. But I didn't want to.

"Seth, the office wing should be right here!" I said hoarsely.

"Maybe you just remembered wrong," Seth said. "We can find someone and ask directions."

"No, I'm not remembering wrong," I said. "I've been going to see my doctor here since I was ten. The office wing of the hospital should be right where that wall is."

"Here, let's go ask someone."

He practically dragged me down the hallway. He didn't understand. How could he? As we turned right and followed the hallway, I had the strongest urge to cover my eyes. Nausea rushed over me in a wave.

I didn't want to see anymore! Every step, every dated object I saw confirmed what I already knew. This was not our time.

"Seth, everything is wrong," I whispered, too terrified to mention the true thoughts stampeding through my head. If I didn't say it out loud, maybe it wouldn't be true.

Seth didn't seem to hear me. Instead, he focused on a couple of young nurses having a heated discussion at an intersection in the hallway.

"We're moving her into the delivery room," the nurse with frizzy blond hair said. To my frantic, overactive mind, she resembled a rock star in a music video from the eighties.

"The doctor isn't even here!" said the other nurse, who had straight black hair and heavy makeup. She reminded me of a fortune teller. Her large hoop earrings only completed the effect.

"We don't have a choice. She's not doing well. I don't know what else to do. We can't get a hold of the doctor. He isn't responding to his pager. We'll have to get everything prepared so he can just do the delivery when he gets here."

The blond rocker nurse turned quickly and left. Seth and I moved forward to talk to the other one. Before Seth could form a question, the rocker nurse was back, pushing the bed of a pregnant woman who was obviously in hard labor. A man, probably her husband, trailed behind.

As the woman was pushed past, she turned her tired, sweat-soaked face and looked our direction.

I felt all of the blood drain from my face. I tried to breathe, but only a strangled sound came out of my throat. Feeling like I was going to pass out, I grabbed at Seth.

"Hannah, what's wrong? What is it?"

Finally, getting a little air, I whispered past my constricting throat. "Seth, that woman! She's my mother!"

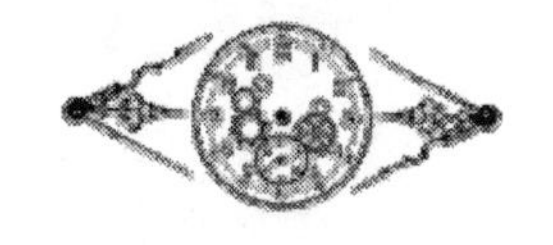

"ARE you sure, Hannah?" Seth questioned. "Maybe she just looks like your mom."

"No, it's her. I've spent all twenty-four years of my life studying her face, her eyes, her hair. That woman is my mother." Feeling panic washing over me, I sat in a nearby waiting room chair and, moaning, put my head in my hands. "It's happening again! I've traveled back in time!"

Seth knelt beside me and clasped his hands over mine. "Calm down, Hannah. It's going to be okay. This isn't like the other times. If you've really gone back in time, I've gone back with you."

Realizing that he was right, that I wasn't alone in this, I raised my eyes.

Seeing he had my attention, he continued. "Now, there

was a man with the woman. Was that your dad?"

"I don't know. I didn't even look."

"I didn't look either. I'll go check. Don't move." Quietly, Seth slipped down the hall to the open doorway and carefully peeked in the room before returning to my side. His own face had lost most of its usual color.

"It's your dad," he said. "A much younger Dan Kraeger, but definitely him."

"Do you know what this means?" I moaned, trying to control the resurging panic. "My pregnant mom is in that room and about to give birth to… ME! Then she will die!"

"You don't know that, Hannah. This could be Abby's birth."

"You heard the nurses. They said she isn't doing well and they can't find the doctor."

Right then, the two nurses exited the room in intense whispered discussion. Fortunately, their whispered words easily carried through the empty tiled hall.

"What are we going to do?"

"I don't know. I guess we'll have to try to deliver the baby ourselves. She can't wait to push any longer. The baby is coming by itself."

"But there's an awful lot of blood already. Is that normal? I haven't sat in on that many births."

The other nurse shrugged. "I'm not sure. She's complaining that it feels like a knife is stabbing her in the stomach. We'll have to do the best we can until the doctor gets here. We don't have a choice."

The nurses continued their discussion, but Seth turned and looked at me intensely. "Hannah, tell me quick. How did your mom die?"

Dazed, I fingered my mom's gold locket around my neck. I hadn't taken it off since Dad had given it to me on my birthday. Woodenly, I replied. "Her uterus tore. They called it a massive rupture. She lost too much blood before they could fix it. They said it was extremely rare."

Whirling, Seth jogged the distance to the two nurses. "Excuse me," he interrupted. "I'm a doctor. I overheard someone is having some trouble. Could I be of help?" Almost unnecessarily, Seth flashed his hospital ID, verifying that he was indeed Dr. Seth McAllister. I don't think the nurses even glanced at it. They were so obviously relieved, they became almost giddy.

"Oh, yes! Please do! We're so glad you're here. Right this way." They practically tripped over each other in their eagerness.

"We have everything you should need already set up. The woman's name is Nicole Kraeger, and I think she's ready to deliver any time."

"Hannah!" Seth called, rousing me from my shocked stupor. "Hurry! I need you."

Following the nurses and Seth into the delivery room, I watched and listened as Seth hurriedly made preparations and gave orders. I followed instructions as Seth told me to wash up to my elbows and put on gloves. It didn't occur to me to question why. My mind and body were numb. I felt nothing. It was almost as if I was observing everything from behind a thick glass window.

"Please take Mr. Kraeger to a waiting room," Seth told the fortune teller nurse. "Make sure he is comfortable and has signed all the papers for us to do any necessary medical procedures."

The young nurse was only too eager to leave the room, practically dragging my dad with her after he pressed a quick kiss to Mom's brow.

Washed, smocked, and gloved up, Seth examined mom. "OK, Nicole, the baby's head is crowning. It's almost time to meet your baby. When I tell you to, you're going to push."

Mom was panting and in so much pain, I don't know how much of her surroundings she actually heard or understood.

"Hannah, come here." Seth positioned me right where he had been sitting. He took my cold, gloved hands and put them on the baby's head. Looking into my eyes, willing strength to me, he said, "I'm going to have to do surgery as soon as the baby is delivered. You can do this."

Leaving me, he started giving quick orders to the rock star nurse, asking for instruments and tools with unrecognizable names. His own hands were busy gathering supplies, making preparations, and checking mom's vitals.

In between his orders and his own near-frantic movements, he tried to give an explanation.

"I would normally have already done a C-section, but it's too late. The baby's too far. I'm going to have to do surgery as soon as the baby is delivered. The birth I'm sure will make things worse, but I don't have a choice right now."

"Why surgery?" The frazzled nurse asked. "Is it the bleeding?"

"The bleeding is not too much at this point, but I think we're going to see a bigger problem after the baby is delivered."

It didn't occur to me to wonder why Seth was posting me in the delivery position instead of the nurse, but in retrospect I could understand his thinking perfectly. He needed to prep for immediate surgery, and he needed the nurse's help to do so. With a panicked look on her makeup smeared face, she was barely managing to follow Seth's instructions to gather supplies in a room she was supposedly familiar with. She kept bumping things, looking in the wrong places, or asking him to repeat his instructions. As inept as she was, I would have had no chance of pronouncing, let alone locating, the things Seth requested. In my numbed state, I was a calmer, safer choice for the baby position and much more likely to be able to follow his instructions.

Mom began writhing and moaning again as another contraction hit.

"Hannah, I saw that Nicole's water hasn't broken yet. In this case, that might be a good thing. We're ready now. If you pinch and twist the membrane around the baby's head, it will break and the baby will come quickly."

Not having time to summon my natural aversion to anything medical, my hand acted as if on autopilot and followed Seth's instructions. Just as he said, the amniotic sac broke.

"Is the water clear?" He asked, not looking at me as he busily monitored Mom and prepped for the coming surgery.

"Yes."

"Good." Focusing on Mom, Seth said, "Okay, Nicole, you need to push. Not too hard. Just nice and gentle."

Seth continued to give instructions as he watched the baby's progress in a mirror on the ceiling. At times, he'd have Mom stop pushing, take deep breaths, and then continue again. I watched as the baby's head slid out a little at a time. "She's coming!" I yelled to Seth.

"Keep your hands on the baby's head, Hannah. Don't push or pull, just support it. The head should rotate to one side as it comes out."

"Yes it is!"

A shoulder came out with Mom's next push.

"Good, Hannah. Now, still support the head, but gently lift the body up towards Nicole's stomach and the other shoulder should come out."

Heart pounding, biting my lip in concentration, I followed Seth's instructions. The shoulder came and then the rest of the baby's body followed easily.

Holding the slippery bit of humanity, I barely noticed the large amounts of blood that followed her delivery.

Seth was constantly moving by Mom's side, not even checking to see if I was following his instructions.

"Keep the baby's head down at about a 45 degree angle

so fluids can drain. Nurse, give her a bulb syringe."

The baby was trying to breathe and cry, but kept gagging. The nurse handed me the requested item, then scurried away like a frantic mouse, continuing to literally run in circles as she tried to gather things for Seth. Suctioning the tiny nose and mouth, the baby was soon mad enough to give a healthy cry. Although I hadn't been aware, at some point, Seth must have cut the umbilical cord. I carefully wrapped the baby in a blanket and held her close.

"Hannah, introduce Nicole to her daughter," Seth said.

Laying the baby in my mother's arms, I watched as tears of joy trailed down her pale, tired face. She lay there for less than ten seconds before Seth was instructing me to take the baby again.

"I love you, Baby," Mom cooed in a weak voice while pressing a final kiss to the baby's forehead. "I'm so proud to be your Mommy."

"Take the baby to her father, Hannah," Seth instructed already administering some kind of anesthetic in a mask to Mom. "And don't come back until I come get you."

As I left, Seth had scalpel confidently in hand.

Leaving the room and walking the short distance to the waiting room, I glanced down at the infant in my arms and felt my breathing stop. She was looking at me intently with eyes that looked as old as time itself. Was I holding myself as a newborn? Were those beautiful eyes, so wise beyond their years, really my own?

Reaching the waiting room, I looked up to see a younger version of my dad pacing the floor.

"I'd like you to meet your daughter," I said, a catch in my voice.

The worry in his eyes immediately softened and as he took the baby in his arms.

I had rarely ever seen my dad cry, but, as he looked down almost reverently at his daughter's face for the first time, I saw moisture pool in the corners of his eyes and slide down his cheeks.

"My daughter?" His own voice was choked up, but not with sadness. A gentle smile of complete joy and adoration graced his face and he pressed a soft kiss on the baby's forehead. "She's beautiful."

Then, as if remembering the circumstances of her birth, worry creased his face again. "How is my wife? Is she okay?"

"I honestly don't know. They had to begin surgery immediately after the baby was born."

Dad closed his eyes as if in prayer, his jaw working as he struggled with his emotions. "She has to be okay," he whispered.

"Congratulations, Mr. Kraeger!" the clueless fortune teller nurse beamed as she bopped into the waiting room. Seeing the looks on our faces, she stopped with an, "Oh!"

"Mrs. Kraeger is in surgery," I explained.

Without missing a beat, the eager nurse offered, "I can take the baby to nursery while you wait. If they had to do emergency surgery, the baby probably hasn't had the newborn procedures and medications?" Phrasing her statement like a question, she looked at me for confirmation.

I shook my head.

"I can take the baby and get those things done," she continued enthusiastically.

Dad looked at the nurse, then looked at the baby nestled in his arms. "Would it be okay to wait until we've had some word about Nicole? I'd kind of like to have the baby with me right now."

Looking as if she might object, I shot the nurse a fierce look. She probably assumed, since I'd shown up with Seth and helped him, that I was some kind of nurse too. At any rate, she wilted under my look and immediately became conciliatory. "Sure, that would be fine. Could I get you anything? If you want, I could bring some formula for the baby in case she gets hungry before your wife can feed her."

"Thanks. I'd appreciate that," Dad replied, relieved.

As the nurse left the room on her errand, Dad took a chair, and I sat across from him.

Palms sweating, heart thumping, I decided I had to know for sure.

"Does the baby have a name?" I asked.

Dad smiled. "Her name is Abigail Nicole."

Abby! I was stunned. I had delivered Abby! "But," I asked, trying to sort out the confusion in my head. "Do you have any other children? Another daughter?"

"No. Abby is our first."

How was this possible? Had Mom had complications

with Abby's birth as well? My head hurt with the effort of trying to think through the possibilities. No scenario seemed to fit.

I suddenly remembered that today was Abby's birthday in our current time. She and Tom were in the Caribbean, and Dad and I had been going to try to call her when I arrived at his house. Now that I thought about it, I realized that, when I'd time traveled previously, I had always gone back to the same day as my current time, just a different year. It now made sense that it would be Abby's birth that I'd just witnessed. But, I was still confused about the complications Mom was having.

The fortune teller nurse returned, interrupting my muddled thoughts and leading a harried-looking older man. The doctor had finally arrived.

Thinking Seth might need some backup, I discreetly followed as the nurse and doctor entered what was the current operating room.

"What do you think you're doing!" I heard the doctor shout.

I didn't hear Seth's response, and I couldn't understand most of the heated argument that followed.

Seth rarely got angry, and I don't know that I'd ever heard him raise his voice before, but the argument finally ended when I heard Seth clearly shout. "I'm saving this woman's life! Either do what I say or GET OUT!"

Judging by the silence, the tardy doctor had decided on option number one. I made it back to the waiting room before a pale fortune teller nurse bustled back out to continue other errands.

Minutes crawled by as I waited with Dad. The only movement from the room was the rock star nurse's frequent trips for supplies, but she never said anything to us. Dad and I alternated silence with small talk. The baby got fussy, and Dad awkwardly but determinedly fed her the formula the nurse had brought. Watching Dad try to diaper a baby for the first time would have been hilarious under less stressful circumstances. I'd offered to help or just do it myself, but he was determined to take care of his baby girl himself. Eventually, he was about to figure the diaper out and strap it on with only minimal instructions on my part.

At one point, Dad asked me to fill him in on the details of Abby's birth. Trying to eliminate the graphic, I simply said that I had delivered the baby while the doctor was making preparations for the surgery. I also told him about the touching moment when Mom had gotten to hold Abby. I didn't feel the need to tell him that I wasn't actually a nurse. I just let him assume that I was. I also had to work very hard at not calling him 'Dad' or conversing in a way that would reveal how much about him I actually knew. Several times, I had to bite my tongue as I started to mention Grandma or something that hadn't happened yet.

Well over an hour after I'd placed Abby in Dad's arms, he was pacing again when Seth finally appeared, his face pale and weary.

"Mr. Kraeger, your wife made it through surgery, and I believe she will be fine." Immense relief washed over Dad's face. "She had a very large tear in her uterus. It was a miracle that she was able to deliver a live, healthy baby. Nicole came very close to dying herself. I am sorry to tell you that the only way I was able to save her life was to do an emergency hysterectomy."

The room started spinning. I sat down on a chair before I passed out.

"No more children," Dad whispered hoarsely.

"Seth… " I croaked out. "The baby's name is Abby. Abigail Nicole."

Shock and horror painted Seth's eyes. "You mean…? Mr. Kraeger, do you have any other children? Another daughter?"

"No," Dad replied, looking a little confused that this was the second time someone seemed to expect him to have another child. "Abby is our first… and, I guess,… only child."

"She was dying," Seth explained, trying to make sense of things. "Doing a hysterectomy was the only way I could save her. As it is she's lost a lot of blood and is very weak."

"I understand," Dad said, assuming Seth was trying to justify his actions for his benefit.

"I'm not sure you do understand," a new voice entered the conversation, and I turned to see the tardy doctor. "Mr. Kraeger, I'm going to be blunt with you. Your wife should have died. I have examined her and realize, even if I had been here, I'm not sure I could have saved her. I am a family physician, but, after watching Dr. McAllister, I can assure you that he is a very skilled surgeon. He is the only reason your wife is alive."

Dad was choked up and could barely speak. "I don't know how to thank you, Dr. McAllister. You and your nurse, Hannah, gave me my wife and child. If I can ever do anything for you…"

Seth, feeling awkward with the praise, accepted Dad's thanks with a nod, then said with a slight smile. "I'll remember your offer and might take you up on it someday."

"Mr. Kraeger," the other doctor said," why don't I show you to the nursery and then take you to your wife's room? She's being moved right now, and I believe we still need to do some work with your little one."

Anxious to see Mom, Dad left quickly with the doctor, leaving Seth and me alone. He perched next to me on the lumpy couch.

"Am I going to disappear now, cease to exist?" I asked him fiercely. "Mom and Dad will never have another baby! I will never be born!"

"She would have died, Hannah! You heard the doctor. He's right! In order to stop the bleeding, I had to use a technique for the hysterectomy that hasn't been invented yet! If we hadn't been here, your mother would have died. She wouldn't have been able to give birth to you anyway!"

"How do you know? Your specialty isn't obstetrics." I hated myself for saying it even as the words came out. I knew Seth was an exceptional doctor, and I didn't want to question his knowledge or ability. So many emotions were tumbling through me that I couldn't seem to stop the anger and the words.

"No, it isn't," Seth said, apparently not taking offense. "But that doesn't mean I don't know anything about it. I've studied all areas of medicine. The only reason I knew how to do the hysterectomy differently was because Natalie told me about the new methods. She'd seen a video and was quite impressed. You know I'm curious about any new research and techniques, so I read some articles, studied up on it, and observed a surgery. But, I never anticipated having to use it on your mom twenty-six years beforehand."

"I'm sorry, Seth. Here I should be thanking you for saving her. I don't know what this means for me. Will I just cease to exist when we go back to our own time?"

"No, Hannah, I'm pretty sure you're safe. The only change I made to the timeline was to save Nicole Kraeger's life. In the original timeline that we knew, she couldn't have given birth to you anyway because there is no way she would have survived Abby's birth."

"I don't understand. If all that is true, where did I come from?"

"The only possible explanation I can think of is that Nicole Kraeger is not your real mother." Seth paused, studying my face to gauge my reaction. Gently enfolding my hand in his, he continued, "Is it possible that you had the same father but a different mother than Abby?"

"No!" I said vehemently. "You know my dad, Seth. He hasn't even looked at another woman since mom died. Not to mention his high personal code of ethics. There's no way he'd have a love child with another woman. Abby and I are barely two years apart."

"Well, then, is it possible that you were adopted?"

Instead of voicing the instant denial on my lips, I made myself stop and think about it. Searching my memories, I couldn't find even the smallest clue or inconsistency. "I don't think so. I've seen the baby pictures from when I was tiny. I've always been told that Mom died when I was born. Besides, everyone has always said how much Abby and I look alike."

"I'm sorry, Hannah, but you've been lied to on some level. Your mom didn't live to see Abby turn a day old. Your family has to know more than they've told you."

It felt as if somebody had just told me that, instead of being clothed in beautiful clothes, I was actually naked. Everything I knew about my life now seemed skewed, my world turned upside down.

"Who am I?" I whispered brokenly.

Gently lifting my quivering chin and meeting my tear-blurred eyes, Seth said, "You're mine. No matter the circumstances of your birth, that doesn't change the person you are today. We'll figure this out. When we get back to our own time, I'll help you get some answers."

Resting my head on Seth's shoulder, he held me in silence for a few moments, gently smoothing my hair away from my wet face.

Finally, leaning back, he said. "Now, how does this work? It's getting late, and we can't stay here in the hospital. How do we get back to our own time?"

Giggling slightly hysterically, I replied, "I wish I knew! I've never figured out a special recipe or spell. It just sort of happened before, but I have no idea how."

"That's not good." Thinking and running a hand through his hair, Seth concluded, "I guess we'll just have to stay here at the hospital until they kick us out. I somehow doubt any hotel will accept my credit card that doesn't expire for twenty-seven years, and I have a pitiful amount of cash on me."

Sitting in silence for a few moments, just waiting and hoping to be whisked into the future, I finally acknowledged my growling stomach. "How much cash do you actually have? I'm starving."

"I'm hungry too. I probably have enough to make a good raid on a vending machine, provided it isn't too picky about the date on the currency. Wait here. Man go out, kill processed sugar and fat, bring back to woman." Winking, Seth left on his hunting trip.

Feeling a hand on my shoulder, I jumped. I'd been so deep in thought I hadn't noticed Seth return.

"Chocolate to the rescue," he said, dropping a couple of candy bars and a bag of M&Ms on my lap. Bless that man! You gotta love a man who understands your need for chocolate.

"What were you thinking about just now?" Seth asked, opening a Snickers bar. "I didn't mean to startle you."

"I was thinking about everything that's happened today," I answered. "It isn't every day that you deliver your older sister."

Seth reached over and held my hand. "Did I mention how proud I am of you? I know how much you dislike anything medical. Besides the fact that it was your mom who was in labor and you were delivering your sister, you kept calm and did everything perfectly. You were my brave Hannah, yet again."

I blushed slightly, embarrassed by his praise. "It actually

didn't bother me as much as I would've thought. Usually blood makes me squeamish and the thought of having to deliver a baby might give me a panic attack. I guess I was just so in the moment, knowing that so much depended on me, that I didn't have time to think about what I was really doing."

"I couldn't have done it without you."

"The whole experience has kind of got me thinking. I've always avoided medicine, but maybe I should think about going into the medical field. I certainly didn't have a problem today. Maybe I could become a nurse and help you and Wayne at your new research clinic."

Seth tried to hide his smile, but I saw it anyway. "We'd be glad to have you, but I'm not sure you'd enjoy being a nurse." At my confused look, he explained. "You have your insecurities, Hannah, but, for the most part, you're way too bossy and opinionated to be a nurse. You'd be happier being a doctor. That way, you wouldn't have to follow orders."

I made a face. "I don't know that I want to go through all of the trials of medical school and residency that you went through. I'm not *that* dedicated to medicine." I sighed. "Maybe I could just help you and Wayne out with receptionist work and the financial side of things."

"Hannah," Seth said seriously, putting a hand on either side of my face and making me look at him. "You can do anything you want. You are smart and talented enough that you can be anything. If you want to be a nurse, doctor, receptionist, artist, teacher, astronaut, or acrobat, just do it! You're going to be successful no matter what you do!"

"You sound like my dad. He always told me I could do

anything I set my mind to."

"Smart man."

"Except now I'm not even sure he is my dad. At the very least, he hasn't been honest with me. He's let me believe a lie."

"He is your dad in every way that counts. If he kept something from you, I'm sure he had his reasons. Don't worry; we'll figure things out when we get back to our own time."

"But what if we don't get back? What if I never find out the truth?" Feeling too nervous to sit anymore, I stood and began pacing the floor.

"Relax, Hannah." Seth stood, and putting his hands on my shoulders, stopped my pacing. "Even if we don't get back, what's the worst that could happen?"

"I'd disappear and cease to exist because you prevented my mom from ever being able to conceive me."

Seth rolled his eyes. "Besides that. I already explained why that wasn't going to happen. You're safe."

"Well, I guess the next worst thing that could happen is that we could get stuck in this time and never go back to twenty-six years from now."

"Even if that does happen, it wouldn't be so bad. You wouldn't be alone. We'd have each other. At the very least, I could make a killing on the stock market and wagering on games."

"You hate gambling."

"I don't think you can call it gambling when you already

know what's going to happen. That's just winning, and I could like that a lot."

Barely smiling at Seth's attempt to lighten the situation, Seth sighed and turned serious. "Hannah, we'll be okay. If we never go back to our own time and you have to relive some horrific fashion trends of twenty years ago, we'll adapt and make it. We'll be together."

Seth lightly touched my forehead, trying to smooth the lines of worry. "This is hardly a desert island, but if I was stranded on one, the person I'd want there with me is you. In my mind, this isn't a bad situation. I much prefer being in this time with you, than in my own time without you."

I reached up and lightly stroked his jawline, feeling the stubble of his five o'clock shadow. "Thank you, Seth."

Pulling me close, he buried his face in my hair. I shut my eyes, relishing the feel of his strong arms around me. The lingering scent of aftershave on Seth's skin was better than any aromatherapy, and I felt my muscles slowly release their tension as I finally believed that, no matter what happened, Seth and I would be okay.

"Remember, Hannah?" His whispered breath against my ear sent goosebumps down to my toes, and my heart started missing beats as I strained to hear his words. "I love you."

I raised my eyes to his and parted my lips, "I lo…"

"Excuse me," an overly loud voice interrupted. "Can I help you two with something? Our visiting hours were over a while ago."

A rather sour-faced older lady in lime green scrubs raked us with an accusing glare.

Embarrassed, I scanned the room for the nearest exit. Feeling a bolt of electricity shoot through me, I realized that, once again, everything was different. All of the furniture was newer and the paint and décor more modern. There was even a TV in the corner. Looking back to Seth, I met his own knowing grin.

Then the pain hit like a freight train.

Grabbing my head, I think I may have screamed, but I don't know for sure. The sudden pain and nausea were excruciating. It felt as if my head was on fire and splitting open. Swaying with pain and dizziness, I felt Seth's arms catch me and heard his voice yelling at the nurse. Mere seconds felt like hours, and, when I was sure I couldn't take anymore, I found the blessed relief of black nothingness.

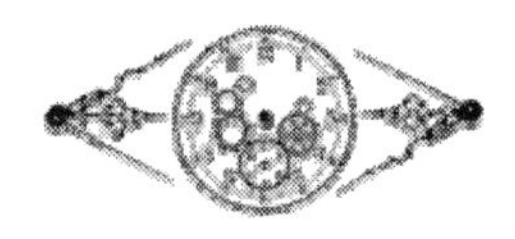

CHAPTER THREE

I'VE never been claustrophobic. In fact, I kind of like close, dark places. Growing up, I would hide in my closet when I got upset. It used to drive Dad and Abby nuts, but I found the dark silence calming and comforting. So now, finding myself in a thick, dark cocoon, I liked it and had no desire to leave.

Every once in a while, I would surface a little, the black would become gray, and I was able to hear voices and beeping noises. But then, the pain would hit, and I would dive back down to where thoughts, worries, and pain didn't exist.

I became aware of one voice more than others. At some point, I recognized it as Seth's, and I honestly wished he'd stop talking so much. His voice reached down and disturbed my pleasant nothingness. Wanting to get him to be quiet, I struggled to understand his words. To my shock, I realized they sounded angry.

"Wake up, Hannah! I'm not going to let you give up. Fight! It's time for you to wake up! Where is the brave, stubborn Hannah I love?" His tone of his words changed from anger to anguish. "Come on, Hannah. You can't put me through this anymore. I need you."

After pausing for less than five seconds, Seth began another tirade. "Hannah, you're not being fair. I know you could fight and wake up if you really wanted to. You're not in a coma. You can probably hear every word I say…"

"Shut up, Seth," Eyes still closed, I managed to grate the words out past my dry, unused throat.

"What?" Seth practically squeaked the word, obviously not expecting me to actually respond to his monologue.

"Just be quiet. No more talking."

"Hannah, you're awake!"

Knowing that he really wouldn't be quiet now, I hesitantly opened my eyes, realizing the pain in my head was bearable now. Scanning the orderly room, I recognized that I was in a hospital.

"How are you feeling?" Seth asked, checking the monitors beside me and looking into my eyes with an annoying bright light. Despite his enthusiastic examination, Seth looked terrible. His face was pale and dark circles framed eyes that held little of their usual sparkle.

"Better. I'm in a hospital?"

"Yes. After you passed out, we couldn't revive you and your vitals were unstable. I insisted that you be transferred here to San Francisco by helicopter."

"Did you tell them about the time traveling?" I knew that a hospital meant tests and unfamiliar doctors, which immediately pushed my panic button.

Seth's eyes flew wide, and he quickly caressed my cheek and reassured. "No, Hannah, stay calm. Everything is fine. Wayne was waiting to help when we arrived. He and I have been the only doctors to treat you. As far as everyone else knows, you're under our care and there was no apparent precipitating cause to your strange blackout."

Seeing me rub my temples, Seth offered me some over-the-counter painkillers. "We had been giving you stronger medicine for the pain, but we took you off it when we thought it might be preventing you from waking up. Your scans showed that you weren't in a coma, and based on your last experience, I thought it had been more than long enough for some of the effects to start wearing off."

"How long has it been?"

"Two and a half days."

It was unnerving to realize I'd completely missed two days of my existence. It had taken less than twenty-four hours for me to start to feel better last time. The difference was more than a little scary.

"You had me worried, Hannah." Seth smiled a little. 'Sorry about the talking." I didn't know what else to do."

The door opened before I could respond, and Wayne walked in.

"She's awake!" he said enthusiastically. "So I guess all your talking worked, Seth."

"He wouldn't shut up," I complained, only half joking.

"Well, since kissing my Sleeping Beauty obviously wasn't working, I had to resort to stronger methods," Seth teased.

Wayne repeated the exact same annoying examination of my eyes and vitals that Seth had just completed. Apparently satisfied, Wayne offered, "I suggested Seth give a different prince a shot at the kissing thing, but he wasn't really in favor of that idea."

Much to my amusement, Seth actually glared while Wayne adopted an overly innocent look.

"What?" Wayne asked with mock indignation. "Don't look at me like that, McAllister! I offered purely in the interest of medical science."

"Yeah, right." Seth scoffed. "Like you'd advocate any medical treatment unless you had a test to back you up. I certainly don't recall any of Hannah's tests indicating THAT would be an appropriate remedy."

"Tests?" I asked, interrupting their playful argument as my mind centered on the ugly word. "What tests?'

Now it was Wayne's turn to shoot a glare in Seth's direction, as if he wished Seth hadn't mentioned anything.

Not receiving an immediate response from either doctor, I questioned again with more urgency. "You have to tell me. Did you find out anything?"

"Yes and no," Seth finally answered. "We still don't know for sure why you time travel, but we do have a pretty good handle on the physical effects it's having on your body."

"I'm listening." Although I hadn't wanted tests, now that they were done, I definitely wanted the results.

"I already said that your vitals were unstable when you first arrived at the hospital. We immediately did both a CT scan and an MRI, as well as panels of blood work. I know you really didn't want testing, Hannah, but we didn't have a choice."

"It's okay, Seth. I'd already told you I'd have testing done, remember?"

As Seth smiled and squeezed my hand to indicate that he did remember why I had finally changed my mind about the testing, Wayne took over the report.

"The CT and MRI were normal, so we did a Positron Emission Tomography. This PET scan, on the other hand, was extremely abnormal. Usually, chemical levels in the brain cannot be accurately measured with a blood test, but we tried anyway. The only abnormality we found initially was an extremely high level of a certain chemical called tempamine. It's a neurotransmitter similar to serotonin, but it isn't a chemical that we normally see variance in. The levels in your blood were literally off the charts. Honestly, there is no medical record we could find of anyone ever having an elevation of tempamine, especially nothing to the degree that you did. There is no way to be absolutely certain, but we think this extremely high tempamine level was what we saw on your abnormal PET scan."

Seth continued, "We think this also caused your intense headache, nausea, and even the blackout."

"But we had no idea how to treat it," Wayne said.

"Then how did I recover?"

"You recovered on your own," Wayne said with an obvious satisfaction that I didn't understand. "Just like you did the previous two times. It just took your body longer this time."

Seth explained, "You'll have to excuse Wayne's gloating. We disagreed on how to treat you, and he feels that he was right. But, there really isn't any way of telling if my methods would have led to a quicker recovery."

"Give me a break, McAllister." Wayne said. "You can't admit that I was obviously right?"

Seth ignored Wayne and continued explaining. "I wanted to try some medications, similar to anti-depressants, which can be used to control chemicals in the brain."

"I said that, given the extremely high levels, there was no way any of those medications could bring them down. It would be a drop in the bucket. Not to mention, the medications could interfere with what your body was already trying to do to repair itself. Given that you had recovered twice previously, I thought we should give your body a chance to right itself again."

"Wait a minute," I interrupted. "I hate that you two argued over my treatment. You're friends, and you're working toward being partners. I don't want to interfere with any of that."

Both men looked at me blankly as if I was speaking a foreign language. Suddenly, Seth started laughing and Wayne soon joined him.

"Hannah, you don't understand." Seth said. "The fact that we argue over treatment is exactly why we want to be partners."

"You've heard the phrase, 'Steel sharpens steel'?" Wayne asked. "Why would I want to have a partner who always agreed with me? We don't argue about anything but medicine, and our arguments never affect our friendship."

"But they do make both of us better doctors," Seth finished.

"Well, then," I said, reassured but still a little mystified. "I'm happy that you two can agree to be happy about being disagreeable."

"We are actually quite happy with the arrangement," Wayne said, "and it just so happens that in your case, my opinion seems to have been the right one."

Seth good-naturedly smiled and shook his head as Wayne continued the story.

"About twelve hours after the initial test, we repeated some of the tests again. Already your levels had gone down a little, and we felt more comfortable about giving you pain killers, monitoring you closely, and waiting."

"But this was so much worse than the last time I time traveled." I pointed out. "I was out cold for two and a half days!"

"Each progressive experience seems to leave you with a worse recovery," Wayne agreed. "We think that your body has a more difficult time processing the tempamine and regaining balance."

"So what if it happens again? Will it be worse?"

Wayne looked hesitantly at Seth, but Seth wouldn't look at me or him. He just stared at the floor.

Wayne looked back at me, then said bluntly. "If you

time travel again, Hannah, especially if it's any time soon, you won't recover. You will die. Your body is too weak and won't be able to handle it. You hadn't traveled for almost six months, and still your vitals were all over the place for a couple of hours. You won't survive a worse reaction."

I tried unsuccessfully to swallow the sudden knot in my throat. "How do I prevent it from happening? I don't know why or how it happens in the first place.

"Excuse me, Dr. Hawkins? Dr. McAllister?" We hadn't heard the door open, but a nurse in purple scrubs was now standing in the doorway. "Miss Kraeger's parents are here. They're asking to see her again. They're quite insistent."

"Insistent is putting it mildly, I'm sure." Seth said quietly. Then to the nurse, "Tell them I'll be right out to talk to them. Oh, and please don't tell them she's awake. I'll take care of that."

"Of course," the nurse responded, quickly leaving the doorway.

"My parents?" I questioned, but both men completely ignored me.

"If they find out she's awake, they're liable to break down the door," Wayne said.

"Exactly," Seth agreed.

"My PARENTS?" I questioned again, louder. "Parents as in plural? Parents?"

"Yes," Seth said with a smile. "Parents, plural. As in your dad *AND* your mom."

"My mom? My mom is alive? She's here?"

"Yes, Hannah, I've talked to her myself. Both your parents have been making a regular nuisance of themselves, not wanting to leave your side. You thought your dad was over- protective, but your mom…"

"She's like a mama bear." Wayne finished. "It's best not to get in her path. And definitely, don't look her in the eye."

"Did she or my dad recognize you, Seth? Did they say anything about Abby's birth?"

"If they recognize either of us from that time, they aren't saying. It isn't exactly my place to ask, and it hasn't been a priority. Remember, it just happened to you and me, but for them, it was twenty-six years ago. They also saw us under very stressful circumstances. They may not even remember our faces."

"So, you haven't told them about going back in time or why I blacked out?"

"No. We thought it best to keep it between the three of us for now. If my memories are correct, they were both at the lodge when you came back at Christmas, so they know you've had other experiences. They may have their suspicions, but they haven't directly asked. They know you blacked out and were flown here because of your unstable vitals. They know about the elevated chemical in your brain and that it was decreasing. That's all, but that's been plenty for them to be worried sick."

I nodded. It was still hard for me to wrap my mind around the fact that my mom was alive. Seth and I had changed history. He had really saved her. Thousands of thoughts crowded my head. What would she be like? What would Dad be like, now that he hadn't lost my mom and had to raise two daughters himself?

"Wayne," Seth asked, "can you fill Hannah in on the rest of our theory? Especially about how important it is for her stay calm. I absolutely won't let her parents come in if she can't emotionally handle seeing her mom. They might kill me, but we can't risk it."

"Seth, I hate it when you talk about me like I'm not here!" I scolded, irritated. "Of course I can handle it. I want to see her."

Seth bent down and pressed a kiss to my forehead. "I know you do, my Hannah. I'm just trying to do what's best for you. Wayne will explain."

As Seth stood up to leave, I again noticed how awful he looked. Normally the epitome of a healthy, athletic male, his current pallor was shocking. After kissing my forehead, he walked stiffly to the door.

"Is Seth okay?" I asked Wayne as soon as the door shut. "He doesn't look good."

"He's fine," Wayne replied. "He's just been worried about you. Been at your side constantly, you know."

Although his words were reassuring, the way he shuffled some papers and seemed to avoid eye contact made me nervous.

"He didn't have any side effects from time traveling?"

"He's fine. We think you did the actual time traveling. He just seemed to be along for the ride."

"What do you mean?"

"We have a theory about how you time travel. We don't

know why, but after Seth and I discussed all three of your experiences, we think we know what triggers it."

"Tell me! If we know the trigger, then we can prevent it from happening again!"

"Unfortunately, it isn't that simple. Think about the first time you went back, Hannah. Seth says you were driving up to Abby's. He also said that you're terrified of that road leading to Silver Springs."

"I dislike driving in general and that road in particular," I admitted. "I was pretty nervous about driving in the winter, especially since the guy at the gas station had mentioned the accident that had happened on the road five years earlier."

"So, you were nervous? Scared?"

"That's probably putting it mildly," I said a bit sheepishly. I disliked having people know about my irrational phobias. Thankfully, Wayne didn't comment or seem amused about it; he just nodded thoughtfully and moved on.

"The second time you went back, Seth said you were having an argument with your sister."

"Yes," I admitted, grimacing slightly at being reminded of another one of my less shining moments. "I guess all sisters argue, but Abby seems to have a knack for pushing my buttons sometimes. She did something I felt wasn't her place to do, and it made me really angry. She walked out of the room when we were arguing, and, when I followed her, I found I had switched time frames. Abby felt really bad about the fight later, almost feeling like it was her fault. I tried to tell her she didn't cause me to go back in time."

"I'm not so sure." Wayne said thoughtfully. "You said

you were really angry right before you went back?"

"Yes, I was. But, honestly, "really angry" is probably again putting it mildly."

"So, this third time you went back, Seth said you two had been arguing."

Another bright Hannah moment! Wayne was going to think I had serious anger issues! "Yes, we had been arguing, but then we kind of made up. I'm not sure at what point we actually went back it time."

"Let me clarify." Wayne said. "You were angry at Seth, but then you made up. Was it an emotional make-up?"

By the sparkle in his eyes, I knew Wayne either knew or suspected more of the details of those moments than he was saying.

This time, I didn't answer verbally, but I think my face heating to a fiery glow was answer enough.

"Hannah, don't you see the pattern? The trigger for your time traveling?"

Trying to push aside my embarrassment, I thought about the three times he had mentioned. I was afraid, I was angry, I was furious, but then passionate. Like a light bulb being turned on in a dark room, I understood.

"Emotion." I said, a little dazed.

"Exactly," Wayne replied with satisfaction. "Specifically, strong emotion. Seth and I think that when you experience especially strong emotion, it triggers something in your brain that elevates the tempamine. Normally, people experience chemical reactions based on emotions, but you don't seem to have a shut-off valve.

When it reaches a certain level, it must trigger the time travel."

"But, I experience strong emotion all the time, but I don't necessarily time travel."

Wayne shrugged. "There could be other factors, almost like a tolerance level. Maybe you were overly stressed or tired and your body couldn't moderate the tempamine. Or, maybe these were just the three times in the past six months where you've felt the strongest emotions."

"But how do I get back to the right time? You think the high levels cause me to travel back, but you said the levels were still really high when you tested me back in this time frame."

"You tell me, Hannah. The first two times you got back, you fell asleep or came very close to falling asleep. This last time…"

"I was resting while Seth held me," I finished.

Wayne waited while I processed.

"I relaxed," I concluded.

Wayne nodded. "Strong emotion catapults the tempamine levels, and, with the stress of having gone back in time, they probably stay very high. Finally, when you relax, the levels start to go down, and…"

"I return to my correct time."

"Where your body has to recover from the stress it's been under."

"But, if you're right, I don't have any side effects when the levels are at the highest, when I'm back in time. They start when I return."

"I don't really have a good answer for that, except to say that your body seems to have an amazing capacity to handle the high tempamine levels. When your body begins to work to regulate those levels is when you seem to have the side effects."

Letting all the new information sink in, I suddenly felt the hopelessness of the situation. Closing my eyes, I softly voiced my thoughts.

"If it really is my strong emotions that send me back, I have no hope of preventing it from happening again. So it's just a matter of time before I get upset about something, go back in time, and then die because my body can't handle it. It's not like I can go the rest of my life without *feeling*. As far as I know, they don't have a medication for that.

Wayne gently picked up my hand and rubbed his thumb along the back in a comforting gesture. "No, there isn't. At least not yet. But, you can't give up, Hannah. Seth and I are going to do all we can to figure something out. I can't stop you from feeling, but I've already started doing research to try to develop a medication that could help keep the chemical levels from elevating in the first place."

"Similar to an anti-depressant?"

"It would actually be opposite the way an anti-depressant works. Antidepressants help people who don't make enough serotonin. What we're dealing with a chemical that's in excess."

"You have no idea how long it might take to develop a new medication."

"No. We already have some drugs that can decrease the

levels to some degree, nowhere near what you would need, though. You would also need to have something that you could take on a daily basis as a preventative. Don't worry about it, Hannah. That certainly won't do you any favors. I'll keep working on it. You just need to concentrate on being very Zen."

"Zen and Hannah are not usually on speaking terms," I said. "We actually agreed to go our separate ways several years ago. It wasn't really working out."

Wayne laughed. "Well, you might have to give Zen another shot, just until I develop something to help."

Being familiar and brutally honest with my own faults and idiosyncrasies, I knew, Zen or no Zen, it would be near impossible to keep my emotions in check. I wasn't a drama queen, but I tended to feel everything very deeply.

Turning serious, I sighed, "I guess this is why Seth doesn't really like the idea of me seeing my mom."

Wayne nodded, "Seth is terrified of losing you. He told me that in the original timeline, your mom had died. You never knew her. If meeting her now makes you too emotional, it could be deadly for you."

Before I could reply, the door opened and Seth came back in the room bearing a tray laden with food.

"I thought you might be hungry," he announced, "and since the nausea seems to be under control, I think you're safe to eat what you want.

My food inspection was interrupted by Seth's whispered conversation with Wayne.

"What do you think, Wayne? Can she handle it?"

"I think you're going to have to let her see them. She'll be more upset if you don't."

"I can hear every word you say," I interrupted. "I want to see my parents, Seth, and yes, I can handle it."

Seth nodded. "Okay, I'll let them come in after you finish eating. But, Hannah, you can't ask them about your birth."

I started to ask why, but then I realized that I already knew. The question and very possibly the answer had the potential to be very upsetting and emotionally charged. I really wanted to argue that nothing would happen; that I could control my emotions and stay in this current time frame. But, I knew myself and my wayward emotions too well. Although I desperately wanted answers, I realized it was too big of a risk.

"I won't ask right now," I consented.

"Do you have a sedative on hand?" Seth asked Wayne quietly.

"Right here." Wayne held up a nasty looking syringe on the tray beside the bed.

"I DO NOT need a sedative! If you two don't knock it off and get my parents in here, I just might get angry. And apparently, you really don't want to see me when I'm angry!" Hearing my own words, I sighed and acknowledged the humor that was clearly about to burst from Seth and Wayne. "Great, now I'm the Incredible Hulk."

Trying to ignore their guffaws at my expense, I quickly inhaled my entire sandwich. I hadn't really thought about how hungry I was until the food had been placed in front of me. I knew I must be famished because even the jello looked good.

Hearing a commotion at the door, I turned from my food. Wayne and Seth had been talking while I was eating and were standing in front of the entrance to the room.

"Seth, I've had enough," I heard a woman's voice say. "I'm tired of waiting. I'm coming in to see my daughter whether you like it or not, so get out of the way!"

A petite woman, who didn't look like she could threaten a grasshopper, pushed her way into the room.

"Hannah!" She whispered as she saw me sitting up in bed.

I recognized those soft brown eyes, quickly assessing my condition. In an instant, she was beside my bed, her arms wrapped around me, cradling me close. I knew that voice, whispering words of comfort and love. I knew that sweet smell of lilacs enfolding me in waves of memories. I knew those warm hands gently wiping tears from my face.

Out of the corner of my eye, I saw Seth messing with my IV, but I really didn't care if he was giving me a calming medication or not. No matter how old I got, I don't think anything ever felt as safe and comforting as my mother's arms.

CHAPTER FOUR

HAVING my mom so close sent waves of memories, overwhelming in their intensity. It was a strange feeling to know that I was meeting my mother for the first time, but to also have new, tender memories of growing up with her as a nurturing, loving parent. I knew that, technically, I had never actually known my mom or experienced these memories, but they felt no less real.

I remembered Mom kissing my owies, punishing me when I was naughty, rooting at every game or concert, and encouraging me when I was upset about boys or friends. I knew that even now she was one of my best friends.

Tears continued to stream down my face, the shock and emotions intense. I felt surprisingly calm, though, almost numb. I don't know if it was the medication Seth had put in my IV or the comforting presence of my mom, but I wasn't really worried about losing my grip on this time.

I studied her face, so new yet so familiar. I had gazed at her face in a frame my entire life; now I could see the three dimensional reality I had longed for. I watched the dance of emotions across her face. She was beautiful. Overall, I think Abby resembled her more than I did. They were both very petite and had the same thick dark hair, high cheekbones, and full lips. I did recognize my own fair complexion and, when a slight smile flitted across her face, I thought I also recognized the source of my dimples.

Dad leaned over and kissed my forehead. He actually looked better than I remembered from the previous timeline. He looked healthier and younger, his hair not quite as gray and his blue eyes a little brighter.

My parents made small talk, telling me what had been going on and who had been by the hospital. They seemed to be trying especially hard to stay away from any serious topics. I figured that, thanks to strict orders from Seth, they were probably deathly afraid of mentioning anything that might be upsetting to me.

Finally running out of small talk, Mom paused and then asked rather hesitantly, "How are you feeling Hannah?" Her eyes held misery as they examined mine. "I was so scared. Please don't ever put me through that again!"

"I'm doing better, now," I assured, squeezing her hand gently. "Trust me, Mom, I don't want to repeat the experience either."

"Seth says you'll be released tomorrow if you continue to improve," Mom said with optimism. "Abby is back from the Caribbean and was here earlier, but she left to make arrangements for you to stay in the city a few days while you recover. Seth thought it best to stay close just in case, so she and I will stay to take care of you. We'll turn it into a girls' mini vacation and have a great time!"

"I better be released tomorrow." I said, encouraged, but a little unsure about all the plans that were being made for me. "I don't know about staying close, though. I'll have to get to Sacramento. There's no way I want to miss my gradua—"Before I could finish the word 'graduation,' the math in my head suddenly added up. The stricken look on my mom's face only confirmed my fear. "It's Saturday." I stated, not bothering to phrase it as a question. "What time is it?"

No one answered.

Looking around the room, I spotted a small white clock on a wall. "2:00," I said, reading the time. I paused, trying to form words around what felt like sandpaper in my mouth. I finally managed to whisper, "My graduation was at noon."

The tense silence of the room was broken by Mom's soft, soothing voice. "I know how much graduation meant to you, Hannah. I'm so sorry you missed it, Honey, but we'll make it up to you. We'll throw a big party and have our own little ceremony. The important thing now is to focus on getting well. Seth and Dr. Hawkins say it's really important for you to stay calm and not get too emotional."

Mom really didn't need to worry. I wasn't feeling emotional. I was feeling dead inside. Physically, I felt as if a large weight had settled in my stomach, making me feel a little nauseous. I had worked so hard in college and was proud of what I'd accomplished. I knew it wasn't required to walk in the graduation ceremony, but I had really been looking forward to the experience of crossing that finish line.

Dad piped up, "I hate to admit this, Hannah-girl, but I'm a bit relieved to not have to sit through a big graduation. Our ceremony will be even better than your school one. It'll be a lot shorter and have much more comfortable chairs."

I knew Dad was trying to make me laugh, but it didn't work. I'd wanted to wear my black cap and gown. I'd wanted to listen to long-winded speeches full of clichés. I'd wanted to sit in an uncomfortable chair waiting for my name to be called in an extremely long list. I'd wanted to feel the happiness and pride of my family as I walked across the stage. I'd wanted the entire experience. Now, I just wanted to cry.

My throat ached with suppressed emotion, but I still couldn't manage to find any tears. There was nothing I could do to change things now. It wasn't as if I could go back in time now when I actually wanted to.

Everyone was looking at me with concern, as if they were afraid to breathe for fear I might fall apart.

Taking a deep breath and letting it out slowly, I shrugged and tried to rummage up a smile. "I guess this means I'll have to go ahead and get my Master's degree so I can walk in a real ceremony."

Everyone laughed, breaking the tension in the room.

Seth spoke up, "I guess it's too much to ask what field that Master's degree will be in?"

I only responded by making a face at Seth as laughter echoed in the room again. Everyone was familiar with my legendary aversion to decision making.

My parents didn't stay long after that, insisting that I get some rest. Mom said she was going to check on the arrangements Abby had made, and then they'd both be back to see me later.

As they left, Mom turned back to look at me one last time, concern and love etched into the slight creases in her forehead. It was the same look I'd received countless times before. She'd looked at me the same way when I was six and fell off my bike, skinning my knee and breaking my arm. She'd had a similar look the one night I'd deliberately broken my curfew as a teenager and finally come home to find her pacing the floor. I think anger would have been less convicting than the hurt and fear on her face. It was a look that held love, saying I was one of her greatest treasures, her reasons for existence. It was a look that held fear, saying she was concerned about my well-being. But, it also held a greater fear that she might in some way lose me.

Answering her look with a reassuring smile that I was fine and would be here when she returned, Mom shut the door.

Wayne moved toward the door as well. "Since you seem to be stable, Hannah, I'm going to relinquish the threat of a sedative and go see to my mountain of other work. Try to get some rest. I'll check in on you later."

"Thanks, Wayne."

Seth came and sat beside my bed, holding my hand.

"How are you doing?" He asked, concerned.

"I'm fine. Headache isn't bad. I feel a little groggy,

though. What did you put in my IV?"

"Just a very mild relaxing medication. I knew it would be emotional for you to see your mom, and I wanted to give you all the help I could to be able to handle it."

I disliked having the medication, but I understood the need for it. In fact, I disliked needing it even more. It had been very emotional to see my mom and then find out about missing graduation. I hadn't handled the emotion as well as I thought I should have. I reluctantly admitted to myself that the medication may have been all that kept me from jumping time again.

"Was it strange?" Seth asked. "Was it hard to meet and interact with a mom you never actually knew or grew up with?"

"No, not at all." I paused, trying to find the words to explain the complex memories and emotions. "It's like when I time traveled before, I guess, but on a much larger scale. I have two sets of memories. I have the memories of growing up without Mom, but I also have memories from this new timeline of growing up with her. It's not strange to be with her because I remember all the events associated with this timeline."

"I understand a little of what you mean." Seth explained. "I remember spending a lot of time with your dad in the original timeline, but now I also have memories of the past six months that involve your mom as well. It's very confusing."

I nodded. "For me, my memories are like a picture. All of the memories associated with this timeline are in the foreground. They are colorful, vibrant, easy to see and access. But, in the background of the picture are the memories that I actually experienced in the original timeline. They are definitely there. I can see them and remember them at any time, but they aren't as prominent or intense emotionally."

"That makes sense. But this is the third time you've gone back. The memories from that many different timelines have to be getting jumbled up in that pretty little head of yours."

"No, not really. Everything that has happened is still clear to me. I'm just still a little fuzzy on the mechanics of this time traveling thing."

Seth smiled. "We'll have plenty of time to talk about that later. Right now, I think you need to get some rest. I'm going to go see if I can aggravate Wayne into making some progress on figuring out how to keep you in the present."

Kissing my fingers tenderly, he gently released my hand and stood. I watched as what little color was left in his face suddenly left. His lips moved, but no sound came out. His eyes glazed over. Before I could say or do anything, Seth collapsed.

"Seth!" I screamed. "Seth!"

Pushing every button on the bed, I think I finally connected with the nurse call button. At the top of my lungs, I screamed for help. Shaking badly, I struggled to crawl out of bed and get to Seth, but the confining sheets held my legs like ropes.

The door banged open and Wayne burst into the room, followed by several nurses.

"Wayne!" I screeched. "Help him! He just stood up and collapsed!"

Not pausing to ask questions or assess the situation, Wayne rushed to the counter and grabbed something. Reaching the bed, he didn't bend to examine Seth, but instead turned toward me, his movements hurried.

"What are you doing, Wayne! What's wrong with Seth? You have to help him!"

Before I knew what was happening, Wayne moved aside my hospital gown and plunged a needle into my thigh.

"Stop! What are you doing?"

"Trying to save your life," he finally answered as I immediately began to feel myself being tugged down to unconsciousness. "Seth will be fine, Hannah. If you don't calm down, you won't be!"

Fighting the invisible arms trying to drag me into oblivion, I tried to argue, to ask what was wrong with Seth, but my lips wouldn't obey to form any words and my eyelids were closing apart from my will. Warm, dark waves rushed over me, and I sank into their depths.

When I was finally aware of my own existence, I felt an underlying panic and remembered the need to fight for consciousness. But I couldn't recall the reasons why. I was aware that time had passed and hated the feeling of not being able to control my body enough to fully wake up. I struggled, trying to open my heavy eyelids and move my limbs.

"Shh!" I heard someone say and felt a light touch on my forehead. "Hannah, it's okay. I'm fine. Don't worry. I'm right here."

I wanted to cry with the relief of hearing Seth's voice. Instead, I sighed and easily surrendered to the waves pulling me back down into oblivion.

The next time I surfaced, it was easier to open my eyes.

"Seth?" I called, my voice scratchy.

At my voice, Wayne turned from where he was looking at some papers by the counter.

"Hello, Sunshine!" he called cheerfully. "How are you feeling?"

"Where's Seth?" I asked, ignoring his question. "Is he okay?"

"Seth is fine." Wayne soothed. "Remember, he was here earlier and told you himself. He insisted on waiting until he could reassure you that he was okay. Now, he's getting some much needed rest—doctor's orders."

Ignoring his lighthearted tone, I continued interrogating. "But, what happened? He collapsed. You said he was fine, but obviously he wasn't."

Wayne sighed in resignation. "Alright, Hannah, I'll answer all your questions, but you need to get out of that bed first. If you're being released tomorrow, you need to stretch your muscles and start rebuilding some of your strength."

Happy that I still might be permitted to leave tomorrow, I didn't argue. Quickly sitting up in bed and swinging my legs to the side, my head started spinning a little. Watching me carefully, Wayne held my arms, supporting me as I stood.

"Abby and your mom put some clean clothes in the closet over there. I thought I'd take you for a walk outside in the hospital gardens and see how you do. It's a beautiful day. How are you doing? Are you still woozy?

"I'm better now," I assured, the dizziness subsiding. Wayne reluctantly released my arms, but continued to stand close as he monitored my balance.

"I'm fine Wayne!" I said, annoyed at his hovering. "Get out and let me change! I'll open the door when I'm done."

After gratefully trading the revealing hospital gown for more conservative style, I followed Wayne down the elevator and out the door to the gardens.

It was a beautiful evening. It was clear, the breeze off the bay was warm and mild. All in all, it was an unusually pleasant San Francisco evening. Feeling invigorated by the fresh air, I felt much better physically than I'd expected after being flat on my back for almost three entire days.

Almost as if he could read the direction of my thoughts, Wayne did a preemptive strike. "No, Hannah, you will not be released this evening. I need to check your levels at least two more times before I'm comfortable letting you leave. Your blood levels are in no way a guarantee of the tempamine levels in your brain, but it's all we've got right now to work with. I'm giving you a lot of leniency in letting you come outside, but this afternoon proved that your emotions are still too volatile for you to be released."

I already felt angry with Wayne, and his words only served to further sour my mood. Not one to hold my feelings in, I didn't hesitate now. "Speaking of this afternoon, why did you completely ignore Seth when he passed out? You practically had to step over him so you could stab me with some kind of tranquilizer, without my consent, by the way."

"I'm sorry that upset you, Hannah, but I did what I felt was necessary to safeguard your health. To put it bluntly, you were freaking out. I already knew what was wrong with Seth, but I couldn't take the time to explain and convince you that he would be fine. At that moment, you were the greater emergency. You were so upset, your chemical levels could have easily spiked, sending you back in time again. I had to sedate you to try to prevent that from happening."

Recognizing yet hating his wisdom, I sighed. "Fine. But what about Seth? You said you already knew what was wrong with him? When I asked you why he didn't look well earlier, you obviously lied and said he was fine."

"I didn't lie. I just didn't tell you the whole truth. Seth is fine. He'd already made it through the worst and was on the mend. I think he passed out as his body's response to the recovery effort."

"So, he is recovering from the time travel. He has had side effects like me."

"Yes and no. Seth has had a completely different reaction than you. When you two initially returned, Seth felt fine. After we identified your chemical imbalance, we immediately checked Seth for comparison. Seth's PET scan was only a little unusual, and his blood tempamine levels were only slightly elevated. Soon after, he developed a slight headache and mild nausea. We checked his levels again to find that they were increasing instead of decreasing like yours."

"Because I knew what to look for, we caught it early and were able to give him medication to lower the chemical. It is the same medication Seth wanted to give you, but it works slowly. Your levels were so high, at best the medication would have had minimal effectiveness. Seth's were low enough that the medication stood a chance."

"So, the medication has been effective? Seth's levels are lower now?"

"Yes. They aren't completely normal yet, which is why his body is still having symptoms, but they are much better. Like I said, the medication works slowly, but I think he will probably be completely recovered in about two more days."

I still got the feeling that Wayne might be watering things down a little, trying to protect me. As usual, my mind always went to the worst case scenario. "You said you caught it early because you knew what to look for. What if you hadn't?"

Looking uncomfortable, Wayne looked toward the west where beautiful splotches of color stained the sunset sky. I wished the hospital had a view of the Golden Gate. It would have been a magnificent picture right about now.

Wayne finally answered quietly, "I'll be honest with you, Hannah. I know Seth wants to protect you, but I disagree. I think you need to know everything we know about your time traveling if you have any hope of being able to figure out how to survive. If we hadn't caught Seth's problem when we did and started him on medication, his levels would have continued to increase. In a very short time, they would have been too high for the medication to help. At that point, his condition would have been fatal very quickly."

Shocked and suddenly feeling chilled, I stopped walking and wrapped my arms around myself. Wayne put his arm around my shoulders and pulled me close, trying to offer his comfort and support.

After a couple of minutes of silence, we continued walking, thinking through everything that Wayne had said.

"There's something I don't understand. Seth and I both time traveled. Shouldn't our bodies have responded in the same way? Why the difference?

"Remember when I said that I thought you did the time traveling, and Seth was just along for the ride?"

"But how is that possible?"

Through the gathering twilight, I saw Wayne's eyes start sparkling mischievously. "Think about it Hannah. When you go back in time, you don't travel naked. You arrive in another time fully dressed in the same clothes you left in. The first time you went back, your SUV traveled with you. Now, tell me, at the moment when Seth traveled back with you, were you by chance touching him in any way?"

Clearly remembering Seth's passionate kiss, my face quickly flooded with color. "I'm never aware of the specific moment of time travel, but yes, I would say that Seth and I were… um… touching around that time."

Wayne laughed a little. "I know my expertise on time travel comes mainly from science fiction books and movies, but, in your case, I would guess that anything you are physically touching at the moment you travel, makes the trip with you.

Fingering the small gold locket still clasped firmly around my neck, I realized Wayne's theory had to be right. Dad had never even given me Mom's locket in this current timeline. The only thing he'd given me on my twenty-fourth birthday was the emergency kit for my car.

The locket had traveled back in time with me in the previous timeline and then traveled forward to this changed future, all while nestled securely around my neck. I wasn't willing to give it up, but I realized I'd have to be careful to not let my parents see a duplicate of a piece of jewelry my mom probably still had in her possession.

Again, I was silent, walking slowly and thinking. "I understand the theory that emotion triggers my time travel. I'll even buy that Seth was just along for the ride and that things I'm touching travel with me. But, why do I have the potential for this tempamine imbalance in the first place? Obviously, no one else seems to have this problem. What caused me to be this way?"

"I don't know. There is something different about you. Something that gives you the ability to time travel and causes you to have a different reaction to the experience than a normal person, such as Seth, would have. I already told you that your body seems to have an amazing ability to handle high chemical levels. What I didn't say is that those levels should be lethal. Seth's levels were nowhere near that high, yet they would have been lethal far sooner."

"So you have no idea why I'm abnormal or what the underlying cause of the time travel may be. Do you have any direction on how we might figure that out?"

"No, I don't have a clue. I have some other, more extensive tests that I did on your blood, but I don't expect those results any time soon. All I know to do is to keep working on some form of daily medications that would prevent that chemical from spiking in the first place."

"I can't just wait around, trying to be Zen. I feel like I should do *something*! Would you mind if I looked at your formulas and lab notes? It might give me some hope."

"Sure, I'll show them to you later. Seth said you were pretty good at Chemistry. Maybe you'll have some ideas."

I knew he was trying to humor me. "I doubt that. How long do you think it'll take for you to develop something for me to try? Are we talking days… weeks?"

Wayne winced. "Normally, Hannah, a completely new medication takes years, even decades, to develop, and that's before getting FDA approval. We won't be going through the normal channels, of course. The bad part about that is you'll only have two medical brains, Seth's and mine, working on this thing rather than the dozens we could potentially have. We simply can't risk revealing your problem to even our closest colleagues. The good thing is that, since we're doing this under the table, so to speak, we won't be seeking government approval. The other consideration is that we'll only have one test subject – you."

"So, in terms of a time frame…?"

"We have none. I'm sorry, Hannah, but I don't know how long this will take."

I nodded, feeling tears pricking my eyes. Usually an accomplished pessimist, I was, at the very least, realistic about my own nature. Even with the most advanced and effective relaxation techniques, I knew I wouldn't be able to manage emotional balance indefinitely. At some point, I was going to feel extreme emotion.

As darkness settled like a cloak and a bank of fog began making its ascent from the direction of the bay, our footsteps returned to the hospital. Like our surroundings, my mood had darkened, and Wayne seemed to sense my discouragement.

"It'll be okay, Hannah. Just relax and give Seth and me some time. We'll figure it out."

Despite his words, I still felt like I'd been given a death sentence, and the clock on my life was ticking.

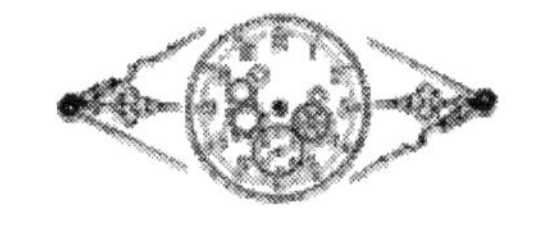

CHAPTER FIVE

I was done waiting. It had been over a month since I'd been in the hospital. Both Seth and I were fully recovered, but we were no closer to finding answers of why I time traveled or how to prevent it from happening again.

I drove my SUV to Seth and Wayne's new research facility with one purpose in mind. One way or another, I was going to get some answers today. After reviewing my options, I had decided that Wayne was an easier target for extracting information. While true that he had been avoiding me, he had already given me information once before. I was hoping that with a little sweet talk or outright coercion, he might again. Seth was supposed to be meeting with a client over lunch, so I knew I would have the opportunity to corner Wayne without the threat of Seth.

It wasn't as if I would be sneaking in or doing something

underhanded. I had been doing a lot of the bookwork and office management duties for the research startup. After Mom and Abby left, I had stayed in the city, wanting to be in close proximity to any potential solution.

I had been staying with Natalie in her fabulous San Francisco townhouse. It had been a fun, relaxing arrangement for the both of us. Sicily had been Natalie's roommate, but she was currently doing a fellowship back East. Natalie was a very social person who hated to be alone. I provided her company. For my part, I appreciated Natalie's fun-loving, no pressure approach to our friendship. She still didn't know about my time traveling or the real reasons behind my recent stay in the hospital, and she never asked. She accepted me at face value and never pushed. With Natalie, I could almost pretend my problems didn't exist. For all intent and purposes, Natalie was my Zen.

As I drove through the hilly streets of San Francisco, I reviewed my plan and what little information I knew so far. I wasn't dissatisfied with the work Seth and Wayne were devoting to my problem. On the contrary, they had been working tirelessly trying to develop some kind of medication for me. Unfortunately, they didn't seem to be making much progress.

Both men tried to be optimistic and pretended, for my sake, that they were getting closer. But I knew they had hit a wall and weren't sure what to do next. At my request, Wayne had shown me his lab notes, formulas, and other research. I'd understood a lot more than he had anticipated or intended. There's no way he would have let me see his research had he realized that I understood everything. Other than asking a few questions, I didn't really say much, letting him think it had all been over my head. Seth, however, had sensed my depression, knew a little of my chemistry background, and had been angry that Wayne had showed me the research at all.

Of course, as always, he was very careful not to show me his anger or say or do anything that might cause me to be emotional. In fact, everyone, including Seth, Wayne, and my entire family, walked on eggshells around me. We had never told my family that I had traveled back in time again, and they never asked or said anything that would indicate they remembered Seth and me from that day twenty-six years ago.

However, Seth had told them that I could potentially have a recurrence if I got too upset. To my surprise, nobody had asked the more probing questions I would have expected, seeming to take at face value that I had some unusual condition that Seth and Wayne were trying to develop a medication to treat.

The result of their limited knowledge and Seth's overprotective warning was a lot of fake emotions and superficial conversations. No interaction or emotion with anyone in my life seemed real. I hated it. It was as if everyone was so afraid of upsetting me that they would never be fully honest or share their feelings. What they didn't seem to realize was that holding back from me was more upsetting than the stress they were trying to shield me from.

Just thinking about it made me tense. The aroma of the fresh pastries in the bag on the seat beside me was driving me crazy. Bringing Wayne breakfast was part of my plan to butter him up to answer my questions. I was a certified stress eater though. At the current rate of my boiling thoughts, the large variety of donuts and other breakfast pastries might not make it the few more blocks to Wayne.

In addition to altering my relationships with my family and my bathroom scale, this limbo status was starting to take a toll on my relationship with Seth. Seth was absolutely driven to find something to help me, giving up sleep and practically living at the small research facility he and Wayne were renting. Unfortunately, they weren't able to set everything else aside and work solely on my problem. They were still doing all the necessary work and preparations to begin their research company.

Trying to manage both priorities was extremely difficult for Seth and Wayne, so they were especially excited when they found a way to combine some of the research for me with research for a paying client. While working on my medication, they had to compare and analyze a lot of different anti-depressant and anti-psychotic drugs in order to try to find some ingredient that might work for me. Inspired, Seth approached a drug company and was quickly awarded a contract to pretty much do the same research and analysis of these same drugs with the end result being that they would be able to use the research to improve or develop new medications.

Seth was primarily working on this contract while Wayne was working another one involving testing a new medication. All in all, the men were extremely busy, trying to fulfill their research contracts, do the work necessary to officially get their company off the ground, and save my life.

The current side effect of this plan was a very stressed, distracted Seth, who didn't have much time for me personally. Of course, he tried to mask his stress when he was around me, but a falsely chipper Seth, who never seemed to give a complete answer to my questions, was highly annoying. I wished he would stop trying to protect me. I missed the real Seth.

As I stopped at a red light, I looked down at the bakery sack beside me. My mouth watered. I could practically taste a fresh donut melting in my mouth. Before my brain could issue orders to halt, my hand was reaching into the sack and connecting with a soft powdered sugar donut. As I crossed the intersection already munching, I knew that the current direction of my thoughts was demanding food more than actual hunger.

I wasn't good at lying to myself. I could fully admit that most of the difficulty with our relationship was not Seth's fault. It was mine. When we did see each other, I was almost afraid of him. I knew I was crazy in love with Seth, I also knew that, more than anyone else, he had the ability to make me feel extreme emotion. My interaction with Seth, whether it had been the anger or the passion, had been what had sent me back the last time. Now, I was afraid to feel too much for him. I hesitated before letting him close in any way. Our kisses were mere pecks on the cheek.

Added to all of this strain on our relationship was the fear and guilt over what I'd done to him. Because of me, Seth had traveled back in time and almost died. He didn't seem to have any lingering side effects, but what if he had? What if I time traveled again and happened to be touching someone else? What if it was Seth again? Would he have a worse reaction and die? The touch that I loved, I now shied away from. Those beautiful blue-green eyes that made my heart race with a simple glance, I now looked away from.

Seth was smart enough to figure out why I was so withdrawn from him, but he never mentioned it. Neither of us ever discussed it. We never discussed anything. I think Seth was afraid of upsetting me in any way, and I was just afraid.

With all of this stress, it was a wonder I wasn't already well over 200 pounds. Licking my powdery fingers and wiping the residue on a napkin, I made the mistake of glancing down. While my white dress shirt hid the powdery evidence fairly well, my black pencil skirt did not. Firmly placing both hands on the steering wheel, I vowed to ignore the rest of the pastries whispering my name and prayed that I'd be able to remove the evidence before being convicted by an observant Wayne.

If only I could get some answers from somewhere, even if it wasn't through the research. But, Seth was adamant that I should not ask my parents about Abby's or my own birth until they could figure out a way for me to be able to emotionally handle the answers. But, much to my frustration, there was nothing in their research that would indicate a solution may be a possibility in the near future.

I was getting desperate. At times, I considered beginning a Chemistry graduate program in the fall so I could learn enough to help do the research myself. I hadn't discussed it with Seth, but I was fairly certain I could pass any tests they required so I could enter as a graduate instead of an undergraduate. If I did go that route, it would be a long time until I'd be ready to contribute anything, and an even longer time until we had a solution. By then, I was sure to have time traveled again, and, at that point, any research or medication would be useless on a corpse.

Taking a deep breath, I loosened my death grip on the steering wheel and tried to focus my thoughts away from the morbid and toward my more constructive goals for today.

The only thing that had kept me going the past month was waiting for those test results that Wayne had mentioned at the hospital. It seemed as if there had been more than enough time for any results to have come back. I had questioned Wayne about them a few times. He'd said that they'd been taking longer than he thought. Last week, he simply changed the subject, and since then, he'd been completely avoiding me. Wayne had been highly reluctant to talk to me at all since Seth had gotten mad at him for showing me their research. Pulling into a parking garage underneath an older office building, I vowed that today I would corner Wayne and not take 'No' for an answer.

After parking, I removed the powdered sugar with the jacket I'd left in the car. Having had previous experience with powdered sugar removal, I already knew that dry material on dry material was the most effective method.

Making my way up to the third floor, I swiped my ID badge through the security system. Seth and Wayne's research facility was actually a suite of rooms in an older office building near the hospital. While the rent on a square foot of space in the city might realistically be out of their personal budget, their wealthy investor's budget was a different matter entirely. This silent partner was currently having a larger state-of-the-art facility prepared for the company, but it wouldn't be ready for several months.

The door unlocked, and I stepped in the front room, noting the mess of files on my desk. Working with two genius doctors had its drawbacks. Both of them lacked some serious organization skills. I had quickly become their crutch. They depended on me to sort through mountains of files and data, read their scrawled notes and instructions, and generally keep everything running smoothly so they could work. Up to this point, I hadn't been putting in full days at the facility as the silent partner's administrative assistant had been handling a lot of the details. But, judging by the current condition of my desk, I figured my hours might have to extend soon.

Ignoring the mess for now, I began looking for my target. Finding him in one of the back rooms in front of a computer screen, I announced.

"I brought breakfast, Wayne! Time to take a break! You've probably already been working at least a couple of hours with no fuel for your brain."

Wayne looked up, his lab goggles still on his head and his eyes blinking as they tried to adjust focus.

"Come on!" I urged. "Even medical geniuses need food! I brought such a variety of breakfast pastries that I'm sure even you, with your sophisticated palette, will find something to like."

"I guess I could take a break." Wayne said, finally seeming to register my presence. "I think I've been staring at this data for over an hour and have yet to encounter an epiphany."

By the time we sat at the table in the small room we had designated for the breaks no one ever seemed to take, Wayne had relaxed and snapped out of his research mode. That's one thing I appreciated about Wayne. He was one of the most highly intelligent, gifted physicians around, and yet that didn't come close to summing up who he was as a person. He was so well-adjusted socially that no one would guess his profession based on a first meeting. Unlike many extraordinary people, he wasn't forever focused on his field. He had a great sense of humor, a fun-loving personality, and could seemingly effortlessly switch between his personal and professional persona.

Looking at the pastries I spread on the table, he asked with wide-eyed innocence, “Didn’t you get a powdered sugar donut? Those are my favorite.”

My face immediately caught fire with guilt. Seeing the teasing sparkle in his eyes, I asked accusingly, “How did you know?”

Wayne reached out and gently wiped the corner of my mouth with the tip of his finger. Holding it up, he showed me. “Powdered sugar never lies,” he explained.

Certain that my face was now blazing crimson, I retorted, “Just be thankful the powdered sugar donut was the only casualty. The entire bag almost didn’t make it. Another two blocks and I may not have been able to save any of them.”

Wayne chose a Bismark, while I dug into a pecan caramel sticky bun. Sometimes, calories are worth it.

“Thank you, Hannah. This is nice. I remember Katherine surprised me once by bringing me breakfast, but I wished she hadn’t. It was a prepackaged vegan quiche she had bought at an organic health food store.” He made a face and shuddered a little. “I couldn’t figure out how they managed to make a quiche without eggs, but, after tasting it, I decided I didn’t want to know.”

I laughed. “How is Katherine doing, by the way? I actually saw her here at the facility a few days ago. Of course, she pretended like I didn’t exist, but she looked beautiful as always. Was she here to see you?”

“No, she came to see Seth. He had some kind of medical

/ legal question he had run into with his research and wanted to get Katherine's input." Glancing at his watch, he continued. "I guess she's probably landed in Hawaii by now."

"Hawaii? And you didn't go with her? You could use a vacation. Seth and I could have managed without you for a few days. I don't seem to be going anywhere at the moment," I said ruefully.

"Katherine didn't want me to come," he replied dully. "It's a business trip, and she said she didn't want to be distracted. She took Natalie, though."

"Natalie? Are you sure? I just saw Natalie night before last. We had dinner together and watched a movie. She said she was going to be pulling a double shift at the hospital, but she certainly didn't mention anything about a trip to Hawaii."

Wayne shrugged, "Have you checked your voicemail recently? I know she's with Katherine. I took them to the airport last night for a red eye flight."

Fishing my phone out of my purse, I saw that I did have a message. Putting it to my ear, I listened. "Hey, Hannah," Natalie's British accent lilted. "I'm off to Hawaii. It's kind of a spur of the moment decision, but, girl, I need a break. I'll ring you later and fill you in on the details. Next time you see me, I'll have a gorgeous tan." I shook my head and smiled. I couldn't really imagine how a tan would look on Natalie's already gorgeous dark skin. She was of African ancestry and probably never saw a bottle of sunscreen in her life.

"You were right. That was Natalie," I said. "But, I'm still confused. I've never gotten the impression that Natalie and Katherine were close. In fact, I'm pretty sure Natalie avoided Katherine whenever possible. And, yes, I think there may have been some choice Natalie-brand phrases reserved especially for Katherine."

"I can imagine," Wayne replied. "All I know is that Katherine is meeting with some of her big-wig clients in Hawaii. Several weeks ago, Katherine said she needed Natalie's expertise as an OB/GYN in a particular case. She offered to pay Natalie and give her a free trip to Hawaii if she'd meet with Katherine's clients and possibly offer expert testimony should the need arise. Natalie said no. But, after working a double shift and losing a patient in the ER, she decided to accept Katherine's repeated invitation and rather large financial compensation."

I nodded. I already knew that Natalie was as sensitive as she was impulsive. She hated to lose patients. She'd told me that was one of the reasons she had decided to be an OB/GYN. She liked bringing new life into the world, and the casualty rate in her field was relatively low compared to others. When she did lose a patient, it seemed to bother her for a long time. That, coupled with Natalie's tendency to make last second decisions, went a long way toward explaining her sudden desire for a Hawaiian tan.

Talking around his third donut, Wayne mused thoughtfully, "I'm afraid, though, that Natalie is going to be disappointed with her vacation. Katherine has a tendency to talk more show than substance—typical lawyer, I guess. She also tends to be a workaholic. Instead of soaking up the sun, they're more likely sitting in some stuffy board room, seeing the Hawaiian sun from behind a glass window.

"By the tone of your voice, I would guess that you and Katherine are off again," I surmised.

Wayne shrugged. Wiping his mouth with a napkin, he then leaned back in his chair and stretched, not seeming at all rushed to get back to work. Finally, he looked me directly in the eye with an amused little smile, almost as if he was calling my bluff.

"Come on, Hannah. You don't really want to talk about my love life. Stop stalling and tell me what you really want. You bring breakfast for me on the one day Seth's out of the office. Either you're ready to give up on McAllister and make my dreams come true, or you want something from me."

As my cheeks returned to their previous rosy tone, I wondered why I bothered putting blush on this morning. Wayne was constantly teasing me over anything and everything, but the aggravating man understood me. He always seemed to read my mood or intentions so well it was unnerving at times.

Returning his straightforward gaze, I said bluntly, "I want answers, Wayne. I want to know what Seth doesn't want me to know."

Wayne sighed and ran a hand through his hair. Then leaning his chair back so it was supported by the wall and propping his feet on another chair, he balanced in a very precarious position. "OK, Hannah. Shoot. You know I've always felt you should know everything, but Seth insists on protecting you. I'll answer your questions the best I can."

"You've been avoiding my questions about the more extensive test results from the hospital. You had told me that it would take a while to get those back, but it's been a month."

Releasing his chair, all four legs banged on the floor.

Wayne bent over, studying his hands. "I got the results a little over a week ago. There'd been some mess up with paperwork at the lab, which is why it took so long." Wayne looked up at me. "Everything was normal, Hannah. I hadn't wanted to tell you because there really was nothing to tell. I had wanted to wait until I had some answers or encouraging progress to report."

"Nothing at all showed up?" I asked. I'd been hoping that some small number would be off and clue us in on some answers.

"Nothing. All the tests I ran for unusual diseases or conditions were negative. Your blood chemistry was perfect. Truthfully, Hannah, I didn't expect anything to show up. You aren't sick. You're the textbook example of perfect health."

"I thought that since something physical causes me to go back in time, there should be an underlying physical cause. Some organ malfunction or gland producing the wrong amount of hormone."

"There may still be something like that, but we're dealing with brain chemistry, a difficult and still advancing field. There may not be a cause. In treating depression, you can sometimes link a precipitating event or physical cause to the imbalance, sometimes you can't. That really doesn't change the fact that the chemical imbalance needs to be treated."

"So where does this leave us," I said, almost desperately grasping at some ray of hope. "My chemical imbalance can't really be treated. Your research in developing a medication for me doesn't seem to be going anywhere. You said yourself that you didn't really have any encouraging progress. What's the plan? Are you wanting to run more tests?"

Wayne sighed. "I think the only tests left to run that would be any value would be invasive and dangerous tests on your brain or DNA and genetic testing."

At my look of hope, Wayne held up his hand. "Wait. Let me explain why we haven't gone down those roads so far. Seth and I would have to conduct all of those tests ourselves. They are expensive and would attract too much attention if we tried to have someone else do them. It's very possible that we could invest a lot of time and energy into the tests only to have nothing unusual show up."

I opened my mouth to argue. The chance of finding any answers would be worth it. Wayne leaned from his own chair and took both my hands in his, meeting my eyes and continuing his explanation before I could fully develop my opening argument.

"Theoretically, Hannah, you could jump time again any day, and then we could lose you. We thought it more important to work on a medication to save your life before trying to do a more in-depth study as to what may have initially caused the problem."

I closed my eyes at the gentle reminder of the timer ticking the seconds of my life away. Only I had no idea when it would tick to zero.

"But you aren't making progress on the medication, Wayne. I know you've been trying, but I also know you've hit a wall."

Wayne looked down, studying my hands still clasped in his. "Hannah, neither Seth nor I am going to give up on you. This is a temporary setback. We'll figure it out. Seth is desperate. He's not willing to lose you. But, what you may not realize, is that I'm not willing to lose you either. I haven't forgotten that you saved my life once. Everything I am today I owe to you."

"I don't know about that, Wayne." I protested, sniffling.

"I do know. I remember vividly how you talked me out of doing something incredibly stupid by sacrificing myself to cover Katherine's drug habit. If you hadn't talked me out of it, I would have lost everything. You probably know that better than I. After all, you did experience a timeline where I did take the fall for Katherine, right?"

I had never actually discussed the original timeline with Wayne, and I wasn't about to start now. Already uncomfortable with his appreciation, I didn't feel like giving him further fuel by revealing his and Katherine's original fate.

I shrugged. "You were in love with her. You just weren't thinking clearly. You wanted to protect her."

"I guess," he said, finally releasing my hands and looking out the small window.

"So, I was right. You and Katherine are off again."

Wayne grimaced. "I honestly don't know. We didn't really have a chance to talk before she left. I'm not sure how I feel anymore. I'm beginning to wonder if I was ever actually in love with her or just infatuated with the woman I thought she was."

"You're just now trying to figure this out? For pity sake, Wayne, that was three and a half years ago!"

"I'm a slow mover," he said, a little sadly. "I guess I'm wondering why I love her when I don't seem to like the person she is. I wonder at times if she's ever truly loved me.

At some point, I came to the realization that she would have let me take the fall for her. If she cared about me or was a decent person, she would have confessed herself. You wouldn't have let me do that for you, would you, Hannah?"

It sounded like Wayne was coming to some of the conclusions about Katherine that I had realized long ago. Biting my lip, I shook my head and admitted. "No, Wayne I wouldn't have let you take the fall for something that was my fault."

Wayne's eyes softened. "You wouldn't let me take the fall for something that was someone else's fault." He gently picked up my hand again, his thumb moving in circles on the back. "Don't worry, Hannah. I'm not going to let anything happen to you. I'll figure this thing out if it's the last thing I do. I owe you that much."

"I wish you'd stop saying that Wayne. You owe me nothing."

"Even if I did owe you nothing, I'd still work as hard, because it's you."

I was quiet for a long moment. Despite Wayne's promises, despite his continued soothing words of encouragement, I felt incredibly discouraged and hopeless.

"Are you okay, Hannah? Or is Seth going to kill me?" Wayne asked.

Not wanting him to know the extent of my discouragement, I masked my emotions by summoning a smile and deliberately sidestepping his questions. "Thank you, Wayne. It's difficult for me to hear that we're not really any closer to a solution, but I feel better knowing the whole truth."

Standing from my chair, I gathered the rest of the pastries back into the sack. "I'd better let you get back to work. I've taken too much of your time already. I know somebody has left me a mess on my desk that I need to tackle."

"Sorry about that. You're just too good at cleaning up after us."

As we parted ways, Wayne looked over his shoulder. "By the way, I know Seth should be coming back any time. When you see him, tell him I need to look over some data with him ASAP. Oh, and ask him to wait until after we get some work done before he tries to beat me up over telling you too much."

"Don't worry, I'll talk to him. If he still wants to beat you up, I'll insist he put it on the schedule and let me sell tickets."

Sitting at my desk, I tried sorting through papers, but found I couldn't focus. After reading the same paper three times without understanding it, I then discovered that I'd just filed a receipt for takeout food with the client contract for Seth's research. Putting my head in my hands, I took deep breaths, trying to relax and reign in my jumbled thoughts.

I was so frustrated! I'd determined to find answers today. I'd gotten more information, but I certainly couldn't say I'd found answers. We were really no closer than we were a month ago to finding out why I time traveled or preventing it from happening again. I was so tired of feeling like my life was on hold. I was supposed to stay relaxed, but how could I with this huge stress hanging over my head? I couldn't take it anymore.

Feeling my frustration stiffen my resolve, I decided what to do. I had determined to find answers today, one way or another. Since Plan A didn't work, I'd have to go with Plan B. Not wanting to disturb Wayne's work a second time, I quickly jotted a note saying, "Gone on an errand. Will call." After attaching the sticky note to my computer screen, I grabbed my purse and my stash of emergency M&Ms out of my desk and headed out the door.

Wayne hadn't been able to give me the answers I'd been looking for, but I wasn't willing to wait around for the next time I time traveled. I would gladly take a risk if it meant getting some information that might, in the end, help save my life. No more waiting.

I was going to see my parents.

CHAPTER SIX

I was my own worst enemy. Seth told me not to worry about the time traveling, about the medication, about anything. He wanted me relaxed so my tempamine levels would stay low and pose no risk of hurling me into another time.

But telling me not to worry was like putting chocolate in front of me and telling me I couldn't eat it! I couldn't sit around worrying about worrying. I couldn't take it anymore. I had to do something!

I had to take matters into my own hands. Seth didn't want me to see my parents yet, but I'd actually been thinking about this for days. I could handle this.

I needed answers.

I knew I was probably being stupid. I knew Seth would be extremely angry. But, at the moment, I didn't care. Along with deciding to question my parents, I took things one step further and turned off my cell phone. I didn't want to hear from Seth. I didn't want to hear his worry and his anger, and I didn't want him trying to talk sense into me.

As I crossed the Bay Bridge leaving San Francisco, I rehearsed what I would say to my parents. I was going to stay calm. I wasn't going to get nervous. I thought if I anticipated and pictured everything in my head beforehand, maybe I could keep my emotions in check.

By the time I reached Sacramento, feelings of guilt had caught up to me. I had gone over the speech and questions to my parents enough that I practically had them memorized. But, now that my mind wasn't occupied, I was thinking about Seth and how worried he'd be over my sudden disappearance. He didn't really deserve this. I'd made up my mind, and, at this point, nothing he could say would change it. There was no way he could physically catch up with me in the next hour before I reached Jackson.

Stopping at a gas station with an attached sandwich shop, I bought some lunch and some chocolate, and I turned on my phone. I felt a little sick when I saw my screen flash the report of 18 missed calls. Before I made it back out to my car with my food, the phone was ringing in my hand.

"Hi, Seth," I answered, not bothering to check the number on the screen.

"Hannah!" His voice sounded tense and relieved at the same time. "Are you okay? Where are you? Wayne told me what you two talked about. I've been so worried thinking you had gone and done something stupid."

Seth knew me too well. I should have known Wayne

would fess up, and Seth would hit the roof. Seth would be able to predict my reaction to Wayne's news of no progress. Not to mention, I'm not in the habit of leaving notes citing unspecified "errands."

"I'm fine, Seth. I'm sorry. I turned off my phone."

"You turned off your phone?" He repeated, his voice now beginning to sound angry. "What's going on, Hannah? Where are you?"

I sat in the driver's seat of my car, dreading Seth's reaction to my location.

When I didn't immediately respond to his question, he continued, "I'll come meet you. We can talk. I really don't think things are as bad as Wayne might have made it sound. We still have several ideas…"

"I'm in Sacramento," I interrupted finally.

There was silence on the other end of the line. "Hannah, stay right where you are." Seth finally responded. "I'm coming to get you."

By the urgent tone in his voice, I knew that I didn't have to explain my "errand." Seth knew exactly why I was in Sacramento and where I would be going next.

"No, Seth. I'll be in Jackson before you can get here. I have to do this. I have it all planned out. I need answers, and this is the only way to get them. Don't worry. I'm calm. I can handle this."

"No, Hannah, just wait for me. Let's talk about this first." The pleading worry in his voice was almost my undoing. Seth wasn't used to being helpless in a situation.

He was a fixer. I hated what I was doing to him.

"My mind is made up. I'll be fine. It's not like I'm going on some dangerous mission. It's only my parents."

"Please, Hannah. Don't do this to me. At least let me come with you."

"It's better this way. I can do this. I'm going to turn my phone off now, but I'll call you later, after I get there."

"Hannah, please." His voice was soft and tortured.

"I love you," a soft sob cut off my throat, and I pressed the End button.

Hands on the steering wheel, I closed my eyes and took deep breaths. I forced myself to relax. I couldn't get emotional, couldn't think about the misery I'd inflicted on Seth. He would be fine. I had to do this in order to have any hope of a future with him.

Giving myself an internal pep talk, I determined to lock all my thoughts and emotions about Seth in an imaginary closet and think only happy thoughts. Starting the car, I turned on a CD of 80's hits, and decided to skip the sandwich and go straight for the chocolate.

Singing at the top of my lungs to Whitney Houston, Chicago, and Michael Jackson, I was at my parent's driveway before I had a chance to think beyond the lyrics. As the last strains of "Alone" by Heart died out, I shut off the car and sat taking deep breaths and gathering my thoughts. I knew my parents were home. They were headed to visit Abby tomorrow and had taken off work early to get packed and ready.

I wasn't planning on wasting time with small talk, I was

going to come straight to the point and ask about my birth. I figured I'd have to tell them about my time traveling and my part in Abby's birth, but, my parents weren't stupid, I thought they'd probably already figured out more than they had let on. They were probably waiting for a cue from me, and I was here to give them exactly that.

I was calm. The fluttery feeling in my stomach was probably from skipping my sandwich. It was a warm day, which would account for my sweaty palms. I was thirsty. That's why my throat was suddenly dry.

Everything was going to be fine. My parents would probably have some simple explanation for my birth. Adoption. Love child. Alien from another planet. Whatever it was I could handle it. I just needed to know.

Finally stepping out of my SUV, I looked at the house where I grew up. Even now, I still looked at it as home. Located out of town off the main road, it had plenty of space. The lots in this area were all five acres or larger, and Abby and I knew every inch of the terrain in a wide perimeter to our own property. The houses in this area were older, but well-kept. The tire swing and playhouse were still fully operational in the backyard, and Dad had just last year applied a new coat of white paint to the modest two story house.

There had been some talk recently of developers buying large tracts of land in the area since the town seemed to be expanding in this direction, but so far, the neighborhood had remained quiet and rural.

This was home. No news my parents shared would change that. Blue frilly curtains still hung in my room upstairs, lines on the dining room door frame still marked the progress of my height, and my parents still welcomed me with love and open arms. Everything would be fine.

I could do this. Taking a deep breath, I took a step toward the house.

An ear-splitting siren split the air. I jumped about a foot and whirled, feeling as if my internal organs had suddenly decided to switch places with my skin. A fire truck blared past and turned at the corner, its siren stopping as suddenly as it started. I looked around for smoke, but saw none. It was probably headed out to help some farmer who was burning weeds or irrigation ditches. That or some passing fireman got perverse pleasure out of seeing me almost wet my pants. There wasn't a lot of action in Jackson, after all.

Heart still pounding, I finally managed to breathe again after seeing that there was no real danger. Hands beginning to shake with the effects of adrenaline, I took deep breaths and tried to control sudden nausea. I really hadn't needed that.

Sighing, I turned back to the house. Only the house wasn't there. I turned around slowly. My house was gone. In fact, nothing seemed the same as it was mere seconds ago.

Feeling faint, I plopped down on the grass and stared.

Instead of my house, a large, institutional-looking structure was in its place. It was only one story, but it was a huge, sprawling building that resembled a warehouse. It had very few windows and was left the gray of exposed concrete.

Having had a similar experience three times before, I was much quicker this time at realizing what had happened. The angle of the road was the same. The shape of the land was the same. Mountains were still in the distance. This was still Jackson. This was still my street. But this was not my time.

Tears prickled my eyes and sobs caught in my throat. I had been so stupid! Seth had been right! I hadn't even made it to ask my parents any questions. So much for positive thinking. I had been in denial about my emotions and the anxiety I felt. I'd had all of my normal physical signs of being anxious—sick stomach, sweaty palms, dry throat—but I had excused them away as having other causes. I had been so determined and wanted answers so bad, I had ignored all the warning signs.

Then, when I was startled suddenly, it must have pushed me over the top and into who knows when. I was an idiot. It was my fault. I might as well have signed my own death certificate. It didn't really matter when I was. If I ever managed to relax and go back to my own time, I would die.

I closed my eyes, trying to assess my options. I had none. I had been stupid. I was currently stuck back in time. I was probably going to mess up the timeline yet again. And, when I fouled things up sufficiently in this time, I would go back to the future to die. And worst of all, I was alone.

I don't know how long I sat there, staring at the building with tears streaming down my face. Mostly, I thought about Seth. I didn't know how I was going to face him. He was going to watch me die. I remembered how his beautiful blue-green eyes seemed to peer into my soul. I remembered the feel of his lips on mine. How I loved him! I wasn't ready to die and leave him.

Suddenly, it was as if Seth whispered "Then don't.

Fight!"

With those words, it was as if liquid strength and determination flowed through my veins. Seth had always believed the best of me. He thought I was brave and smart. He thought I was worth loving. I may have disappointed him in the intelligence department, but I was not going to give up. Even if I went back and landed in a coma, I would claw myself out of the darkness to get back to Seth. I was going to fight until I took my last breath.

Standing from the grass, I headed for the front door of the building before I had a chance to change my mind. I crossed a wide front lawn, noting that a parking lot was off to the side. There weren't many cars in the lot, and, truthfully, I didn't look at them. I was focused on the rather unimpressive entrance and looking for a sign or anything that might tell me what this building was. I didn't recall my parents ever saying that a building had been torn down previous to our house being built, but my parents weren't the original owners, and they may not have known.

Reaching the door, I finally located a sign. In small lettering on the glass door itself, I read the words: Intrepid Research Facility. Beneath the title listed about six names of doctors who apparently worked there.

The door was automatic and opened before me. Not bothering to read the names or pause, I quickly stepped into the cool, tiled interior.

"Oh, good, you're here. Right on time," a voice said at my elbow. My eyes strained, trying to make out the features of the female speaker, but they still hadn't had a chance to adjust from the bright outdoor sunlight.

Before I could respond, the voice continued, "I was a little worried that I had the time wrong. I had to make an educated guess. I'm so glad I was right." She paused, continuing in a thoughtful tone. "Funny, I never realized… you're beautiful."

"I think you must have me confused with someone else," I started to explain.

She acted like she didn't hear me. " Right this way," she said, gesturing to the left. "I'll show you where to go."

My vision had cleared, but the woman had turned to lead the way. I still couldn't get a good look at her face. Not knowing what else to do, I followed.

I took in my surroundings as we went, the woman's heels, echoing hollowly through a large tiled entryway. The interior was about as unremarkable as the exterior. Everything appeared extremely clean, almost like the anesthetic clean of a hospital, but the décor was minimal. The tile was no longer shiny, and the furnishings obviously not new.

The woman stopped at a small reception area at the end of the entryway. A couple of large ferns stood like sentinels on either end of the reception desk and pictures of who I assumed were the doctors employed by the facility smiled from an adjacent wall. A small waiting room with well-worn chairs was off to one side. A TV was mounted in the corner and turned on to what appeared to be a news program.

"Excuse me," the woman said to the receptionist. "I'm from the Tomorrow Foundation. I have with me the young woman I believe the Blakes have been expecting."

As the receptionist picked up the phone to make a call, I

now had the opportunity to study my guide. There was something almost mesmerizing about her. The fine lines around her eyes and mouth were the only clues that she was probably in her early fifties. She wasn't overly tall, but held herself with an erect carriage. She was well-dressed in a classic black dress with a blue blazer and simple silver accessories. She was probably thirty years older than me, yet I found myself envying her hair. The deep auburn color was undoubtedly from a bottle, but it was the color and style I'd always wished for my own hair. Its long waves cascaded in a partially up style that suited her long neck.

Her clothes, style, and mannerisms all said that she was a woman of importance. The only thing that bothered me about this lovely woman was her eyes. They were sad. She didn't act sad. The friendly smile she gave the receptionist was genuine, but there was something about her eyes that said she had experienced a great loss. It probably wasn't noticeable to most people. I only noticed it because I'd seen it before. My dad's eyes had held the same infinite sadness in the original timeline where my mom died.

The receptionist was taking a while on the phone, but the woman never said anything or turned to face me. My study of her was all done from the profile view. I thought about trying to start up a conversation, to again protest that I wasn't who she thought I was. But, honestly, I didn't know what to say. I couldn't really say, "I'm from the future, and I need your help." It wouldn't do me any good to get locked up in a mental hospital in the past. It was easier to go along with the flow until I figured out exactly where this current was leading.

Possibly uncomfortable under my not-so-subtle stare, the woman suddenly turned and gazed rather pointedly at the

TV in the corner. Getting the hint, I turned as well and followed her gaze. I couldn't hear the words very well.

The woman who was speaking looked vaguely familiar. I didn't know if I'd seen her as a news anchor on some program in the future or not. She was probably in her fifties, but she was still a striking blond. She was dressed in what looked to be a red designer business suit that flattered her in every way. The glasses perched on her nose only added to her air of intelligence, confidence, and sophistication. By her body language, I could tell that she was an accomplished speaker, obviously at home in front of a camera.

Finally giving up on trying to hear what she was saying, I began reading the ticker tape running along the bottom of the screen, hoping for today's date or some other clue as to when I was. I read "… reports that government health care is no longer operating in the red. Credit is given to the President's new policies and research funding. This follows the CDC's report of the first overall decline in disease in the nation's history."

"Sorry about the delay." I'd been so focused on trying to interpret the words on the TV screen that the receptionist's voice from behind caused me to jump. "The Blakes were in the middle of some testing that had to be completed. One of them will be out to meet you shortly. I'll buzz you in the door."

"Thank God," I thought I heard the woman beside me mutter with a sigh of relief. "Funny how you never remember how long the waiting is."

I looked back at the TV, thoroughly confused by what I'd read and wanting to continue watching. Nothing I'd read on the TV gave me any clues. In fact, I was more mystified than ever. None of the news reports were familiar. Was I in some alternate dimension or something?

As the woman beside me moved to the door to the left of the reception desk, I reluctantly followed, giving up on the TV for the moment.

I opened my mouth to ask my guide a question, I wasn't even sure what, but I felt like I didn't know which end was up. Before my mouth and my brain could connect, there was a loud buzzing noise and the double doors in front of us opened.

"Go ahead," my guide said. "Dr. Blake will meet you down the hall."

Shouldn't I protest that there'd been some mistake? Shouldn't I beg for her to please tell me what was going on? But, I didn't. Completely dazed, I put one foot in front of the other and went through the doors.

"Oh, Hannah?" At the woman's voice, I turned back around. She looked directly at me, and I saw a full view of her face for the first time. There was something about her that was familiar, as if I should know her but couldn't reach back far enough to remember her name.

Her sad eyes were sparkling with what looked like a hint of amusement, and a smile was on her lips. "Say 'yes.'"

Before I could respond, the doors automatically shut, separating us. Starting to continue down the hall, I suddenly whirled back and faced the doors. *Hannah! She'd called me Hannah!*

I wanted to run back and pound on the doors until they opened and the mysterious woman gave me some answers. I was instead distracted by footsteps coming from the other direction of the long hall. A small woman with bright red hair and dressed in a white lab coat approached me.

Extending her hand to take mine, she smiled, “You must be Esther Jefferies.”

I opened my mouth in denial, but, suddenly remembering the words of my mysterious guide, I found myself replying. “Yes… Yes, I am.”

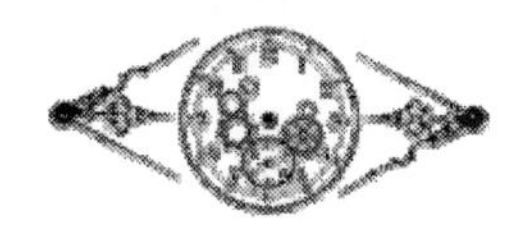

CHAPTER SEVEN

"THANK you so much for coming," the redhead said with a firm squeeze of my hand. "I know that the circumstances were vague and rather unusual, but hopefully, once we explain everything, you'll understand how desperately we need your help."

She was shorter than I was and had to look up as she examined me with a pair of cornflower blue eyes. I could only assume that she was a doctor of some sort, but she was so cute and delicate, she reminded me of a pixie. She didn't look like a doctor at all.

"You're younger than I expected." Right after she said it, she burst into laughter, her eyes dancing. "It's so funny to hear myself say that. People have been saying that to me since I was a teenager! They never expected a girl so young to be attending a prestigious college, let alone be conducting and writing credible research. Funny, now, that I'm thirty-six, I don't get that line nearly so much!"

I immediately liked this red-haired pixie. Friendly people who had the ability to laugh at themselves easily earned a place in my heart, especially since I tended to be shy and reserved when first meeting someone.

Turning back down the hall, she said. "I should know that age in no way correlates to intelligence or accomplishments, and, from what I've heard about you, you have plenty of both. If you'll follow me, Dr. Jefferies, I'll show you our lab and we can get started."

The title of "Dr." completely unnerved me. I didn't believe for a second that I'd be able to pass as a doctor of any field, especially when I was obviously expected to be intelligent and offer valuable help. Wishing my mysterious guide had offered a little more direction than a simple, "say 'yes,'" I felt I didn't have much choice but to follow obediently and hope for divine intervention.

Doors lined both sides of the hall at regular intervals and were each marked by a security box on the doorframe. Reaching the last door on the left, the red-haired woman paused.

"Jason is finishing up some testing on another project in a different part of the building. He'll join us as soon as he can, but we can get started."

Standing on tiptoe to reach the security box, she looked at a little screen for what appeared to be a retinal scan.

Turning to me, she smiled. "I'm Karis, by the way. I'm sure you already figured it out, but I guess I didn't formally introduce myself. I'm Dr. Karis Blake."

Karis. That name clicked in my brain, triggering the memory of an adorable red-haired baby with cornflower blue eyes. That memory, combined with the shock of seeing a retinal scanner in what I had assumed was the distant past, made goosebumps prickle across my entire body.

Where was I?

Pausing for several seconds after she had completed the retinal scan, the door finally slid open itself. Peering into the lab, my mind whirling on overload, I suddenly related to Dorothy in the *Wizard of Oz* when she realized that she wasn't in Kansas anymore.

The room was huge and packed with equipment that I'd never dreamed existed. Computers of all shapes and sizes lined one wall, but they were unlike any I'd encountered before. One screen even seemed to be projecting a three dimensional, full color image. Colorful test tubes and a long work table took up the opposite side of the room, and in the center was large equipment that I couldn't describe. I had nothing in my experience to compare it to.

Awestruck, I scanned the room while trying not to reveal how completely overwhelmed I was. An image of the TV from the waiting room flashed in my head. At the time, it hadn't occurred to me to wonder why a TV with such high definition and strange icons would be in the past. Pausing, I glanced down at the wedding ring on Karis's left hand before posing the question that burned in my brain.

"Karis. That's an unusual name. What was your maiden name, Dr. Blake?" My voice sounded small and breathless.

"Call me Karis." She immediately responded. "Lawson. My maiden name was Lawson."

Everything suddenly came into focus. I understood why

everything was so different. Why I couldn't figure out how a research facility had been on the property before my parents' house. It was there *after* my parents' house. I was in the future. This woman before me was the baby I had met only months before. Judging by her age, I had jumped about thirty-six years into the future.

I had always traveled to the past, and it had never occurred to me that it could happen the other way.

I couldn't think. I felt as if I might faint right there on the floor in front of the space-age equipment I couldn't comprehend.

"Why do you ask?" I heard Karis's voice penetrate through my shock and panic.

Scrambling, I made something up, surprising myself at how calm and believable I sounded. "I thought I might have run across something about a Karis Lawson before, and I was curious."

Karis nodded, the explanation seeming to satisfy her. "I did publish some papers and was known as a child prodigy under the name of Karis Lawson. That's probably where you heard it. The vast majority of my success has come since Jason and I have been married. We make a great team."

"You certainly seem to be very successful." I replied honestly. "I don't think I've ever seen such a well-equipped lab."

"The Tomorrow Foundation has been very good to us, me especially." Karis explained. "They found out about my talents and interests when I was young and pretty much funded my entire education. I wouldn't be where I am today if not for them."

Karis continued, "The Foundation has continued to fund a lot of projects for Jason and me over the years, including this particular laboratory. We have several other fully stocked labs in this facility where we collaborate on other more public projects, but this one is for our own private use. I think only two other people, our mutual friends at the Foundation, know what we're actually doing in here. Even they don't know everything, though. You will be the first."

"Why me?" I asked. If I was going to pull this charade off, I figured I needed as much information as possible.

"Those two friends at the Foundation recommended you as the best in your field. They said you were a personal friend and could be trusted. We did our own research and appreciated your conservative views and high code of ethics. I hope we didn't offend you by asking you to sign that non-disclosure agreement before you came. We had to take every precaution. We're getting desperate. There isn't much time, and we really need your expertise."

I bit my lip. If they were depending on my help, they were going to be disappointed. Opening my mouth to ask another question, I was startled by the sound of a baby crying.

"Oh, she's awake!" Karis rushed over to a crib in the corner that I hadn't noticed before. Bending down, she lifted up a beautiful baby girl. Karis returned to me, holding the baby close, a delighted, loving smile on her lips.

"Esther, this is our daughter. She is the reason for everything: all of our research in this room, our caution, and our desperation. It's all to protect her."

Gently, Karis smoothed the baby's short, wayward red curls. She looked remarkably like her mother—red hair, blue eyes, dimples. She seemed very alert for a baby so young. I guessed her to be two months old at the most. She seemed to be a happy baby, smiling and cuddling close to her mom's neck.

A loud beeping sounded from one of the computers. "Oh, I'd better check that," Karis said. "Do you mind, Esther?"

Handing me the infant, Karis rushed over and began pushing buttons on the computer. I gazed down into the eyes staring back at me intently. Slowly, the baby reached her hand up toward my face. Capturing her chubby little fingers in my own, I smiled down at her.

"Nice try, Baby. I know all your tricks. I'm not going to let you grab my nose. Your Mama already schooled me on that one!"

"She's a beautiful baby," I told Karis as she returned from working on the computer, a troubled look on her face.

"Thank you," she replied, her face brightening. "We certainly think so. You'd never know by looking at her that she was viewed as a danger to the public and the government would prefer her dead."

"What do you mean?" I asked in shock.

Karis sighed. Taking the baby from my arms, she gestured for me to have a seat. Preparing a bottle, she sat in a rocking chair by the crib and fed the baby as she talked.

"I assume you are familiar with the President's new policies?"

Thankful that I had watched the snippet on the waiting room TV, I actually felt knowledgeable to respond. "On the news today, they announced a decline in disease and a surplus in government health care."

Karis nodded. "What they didn't report is how they are actually achieving those results."

Sighing, Karis continued. "Jason and I had tried to have children for years. We hadn't wanted to use any of the artificial methods available today. It was probably a case where we knew too much about them to feel comfortable. We figured that we'd have our own children if God wanted. After a dozen years of marriage, we'd pretty much given up and were starting to look into adoption when I got pregnant. Knowing the genetic testing that is required nowadays, we did our own. We found that, while our baby would have no serious genetic conditions, she did have some irregularities in her DNA."

As Karis continued her story, her expression was sad, almost tortured. "Under the President's no tolerance policy, I would have been required to have an abortion. Jason and I couldn't handle that. We'd tried for so long, and we already loved our little one. So, we kept my pregnancy a secret. Of course, after I delivered the baby, the testing was done, and the genetic abnormalities were discovered. We would have probably gotten in trouble, maybe even been arrested for our deceit, but we provide too valuable a service for the government. As you know, we are among the top medical research doctors in the country and have developed several successful new treatments and medications. Ever since she was born, we have been trying to use what connections we have to save our baby, but, while they were willing to overlook our illegal behavior, they still insist this law must be followed."

"What will happen to her?" I asked with dread.

Karis's eyes filled with tears. "They won't kill her, but

they will take her away and give her a life that will probably be worse than death."

Taking a deep breath, trying to calm down, she continued. "Their true policies aren't well-publicized. The reasoning is that those people who have genetic abnormalities pose a risk to the rest of humanity. If allowed to reproduce, they will pollute the gene pool, increasing genetic mutations and overall disease. You know that the country was in serious financial trouble before the President took over. With the genetic abnormalities out of the picture, the cost of public health care goes down considerably as the general public no longer has to pay for higher than average health needs."

"So is your baby sick?" I asked, thoroughly appalled by both what Karis was telling me and the pure logic of it all. As awful as it sounded, I could definitely see people in my own time making these same arguments.

"That's the most frustrating thing," Karis replied. "She isn't sick at all! In fact, every test we've done on her DNA has shown the opposite. She is extremely healthy, and, if anything, her particular genetic mutations might protect her against many diseases. But no one will listen. They claim they can't make any exceptions to the law."

"You said they would take her away. What will they do with her?"

"People who have detectable genetic abnormalities and are of reproductive age or younger are being sent to designated areas to live."

"Like concentration camps?" I asked, shocked.

"Pretty much. Only they don't call them that or promote them in any unfavorable way. They are special communities fully equipped with doctors who are available to help treat any condition that may arise. People are promised help and a life of ease."

"But you know otherwise."

"Yes. We have visited several communities and been asked to do consulting work for them. We've refused. Remember, people with genetic abnormalities are not allowed to reproduce. When someone new arrives, measures are immediately taken to ensure that doesn't happen. Most people in the communities are not treated badly. In fact, many people seem to like it because they are well-cared for. But they have no rights. They are test subjects. The vast majority of funding for medical research now goes to these communities because they have a ready supply of test subjects and virtually no consequences. While trying to 'help' these people, genetic problems can be researched and new treatments and medications tested. The eventual goal being to improve the health of the genetically pure population. Understandably, the field of medical research is now progressing at an incredible rate. After all, humans are much better test subjects than rats."

I was speechless and stared at Karis in shock. Finally finding my voice, I managed to whisper, "It's like genocide."

"Oh, no. Nobody is killing anyone. We're much too civilized and advanced for that," Karis replied sarcastically. "For the first time in history, disease, population growth, and the economy are under control! Why shouldn't people be ecstatic?"

"So, your baby will be taken from you and sent to one of those communities?" I asked.

"Yes, only it will probably be worse for her than for most. It won't take the researchers long to discover that her abnormalities are beneficial. They will run endless experiments on her, testing and trying to figure out a way to reproduce the same effect with a treatment or medication. We will not be allowed to visit. She will be a lab rat."

"When?" I asked. "When will they take her?"

Karis's eyes were filled with misery. "Tomorrow," she whispered.

"Tomorrow! No!"

"They wanted her immediately when she was a newborn. We have put it off as long as we can. They're coming tomorrow, and they'll take her by force if necessary."

"Send her away," I said flatly. "Send her where they'll never find her."

"That was our first instinct when we realized they weren't going to let us keep our baby. We wanted to find some way to hide her, to send her as far away as possible. But, we realized she still wouldn't be safe, even if we managed to place her with new parents across the country. Multiple tests are performed nowadays to monitor one's health, almost like regular immunizations. Her abnormalities would still be discovered at some point."

"What about sending her out of the country?"

"We would never make it close to a border," Karis said sadly. "With advances in security, nothing can be done in secret. We are watched more than others because of our high profile status, not to mention they watch for that type of thing when preparing to remove a child from her parents. Besides, other countries are not really any better. They're all following suit and focusing on genetic purity."

My eyes filled with tears. "Is there nothing to be done, then?"

"That depends on you," Karis replied, her eyes seeming to assess my willingness and ability.

I swallowed, returning her assessing gaze without flinching. "What do you mean?"

"We've put off calling for you as long as possible, hoping to have a breakthrough. Our connections tipped us off that the authorities will be coming tomorrow. Now we're up against this deadline. We've been working on a plan for a while now. It'll probably sound very far-fetched when I first tell you. What we need is for you to look at our research and give your opinion on whether we should go through with it or not."

"Okay," I replied with false confidence. "I can do that."

The baby was now finished with her bottle, and Karis continued talking as she strapped her into a front carrier. Judging by the ease with which Karis positioned the baby and the infant's happy compliance, I gathered this was their usual arrangement for getting work done.

"There is no place we can send our daughter where she will be safe," Karis said slowly, thoughtfully, as if gauging my reaction to what she was about to say. "But, we might be able to send her to a *time* when she will be safe."

Goosebumps prickled on my arms as my eyes locked with hers. "I'm listening," I urged.

"Jason must have determined this long before I did, before she was born. He didn't tell me what he was working on until it was completed and ready for testing. His idea was that if our baby had been born years ago, there would have been no genetic testing, no purity movement, and no new presidential policies. She would have been safe."

Karis looked over to the center of the room. I followed her gaze to the strange structure that was the centerpiece of the lab.

"You may not know this," she continued, "but Jason has a second doctorate in engineering. A large part of what has made us so successful is Jason's genius at designing and building any equipment we need, even if it's something that hasn't been invented yet."

Pausing, she continued to stare at the structure. Finally, she whispered, "It's a time machine."

Completely speechless, I examined the contraption with new eyes. I don't know what I thought a time machine should look like, but it definitely didn't look like this thing. If anything, this looked like everything in a junkyard had been welded together to create a massive lump of trash. Wires, tubes, and unidentifiable objects extended chaotically from a center unit. Most of it was constructed of a material that I had never seen before. It was shiny like metal, but almost translucent.

Taking a deep breath, I turned back to Karis, who was closely monitoring my reaction. If Jason had built a time machine, and they wanted my opinion on it, I may be much more uniquely qualified than I ever imagined. Maybe this was the reason I was here. I could help someone again and possibly help save a child's life.

"How can I help?" I asked

Karis beamed. "Thank you. I'll show you the actual

research and explain the problems we've been having."

I followed as Karis walked over to the computers, the baby gurgling happily with the ride.

"We've tested the machine on multiple occasions," Karis said. "It works. What we need from you is an honest assessment of whether our daughter will be safe making the time travel."

"How far are you planning to send her back?" I asked.

"Fifty-nine years. She should be safe then. There was no mandatory genetic testing at that point."

"But won't she have to face some of the same problems once she's old enough to reach this time?"

"Yes and no. So far, the government is leaving people alone if they are over reproductive age. Of course, there's a chance that eventually the discrimination will reach the older ages."

"Also, what if your daughter has children? What if they have the same genetic abnormalities? They'll face the same problem when their timeline reaches this point."

"As you know, you can't guarantee genetics. It's possible her children will be completely normal. This mandatory testing and relocation is very recent, only beginning with this latest administration. Jason and I are also working on some other projects that should insure the safety of babies born in the future. One of our public projects is to develop a way of fixing genetic problems before a child is born. Privately, we're also working on a medication that will mask any genetic abnormalities. Anyone who takes this medication before testing will show up as having a perfect genetic code. We're a lot closer to developing a masking agent. If we had more time, it could be used for our current situation."

"So, you're going to have to give up your daughter to a different time."

Karis looked down at the wiggly bundle in front of her and tried to blink away tears. "At least this way she'll have a chance at a normal healthy life. I keep telling myself it won't be forever. Eventually, she will reach this time again and maybe we'll get to meet her. Of course, at that point, we'll also be ready to help her or her children should the need arise. She'll be much older than me when that happens, but I won't care. I'll still love her."

My heart ached with the sacrifice Karis was making. I wished I could find a way so she could raise her daughter. The fact that she was willing to give her up to protect her showed the surpassing love she held for that red-haired baby.

"Fifty-nine years." I mused quietly. "That's a pretty specific number."

"Yes, it is. We've done a lot of research and determined that it would be the absolute best time to send her to. Before this research facility was here, this was a residential neighborhood. Looking at old blueprints, we've determined that this room was a family's backyard. From what we've determined, they seem like an exceptional family, the kind we'd want to raise our daughter. They even have a daughter who will be about two years older than ours. Everything is ready. We've drawn up adoption papers current for fifty-nine years ago to make everything appear legal if they are ever questioned. We've written letters asking them to care for and love our baby as if she was their biological child. While not giving all the details as to why we sent her, we've outlined specific instructions on how to proceed. We have every detail ready. All we are waiting for is your assessment."

As Karis spoke, I felt my throat constricting. I couldn't breathe. I practically collapsed into a chair, staring at her. She didn't seem to notice my reaction, focusing on bringing up some files for me to look at on the computer.

"What is the family's name?" I finally asked in a strangled whisper.

"Kraeger." Karis responded. "Dan and Nicole Kraeger."

Numb. I couldn't think. My eyes met the baby's. She stared at me intently, and I stared back. A blue reflection.

"Karis," I asked quietly. "I don't think you ever told me your daughter's name."

She looked lovingly down at the baby, smiled gently, and replied. "Her name is Hannah."

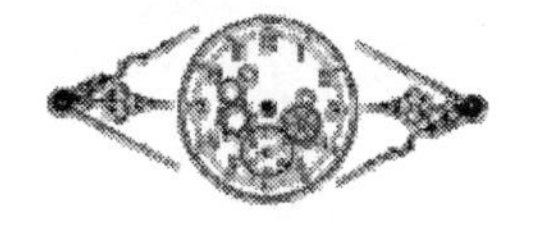

CHAPTER EIGHT

I don't know why I hadn't seen it before. I had seen pictures of myself as a baby. I thought I remembered seeing pictures of myself as a newborn. I guess no one actually expects to meet herself. Now, however, there was no question in my mind that the baby nestled against Karis was me. Karis, the yet unborn daughter of the couple I had rescued less than a year ago, was my MOTHER!

With hearing my own name from Karis's lips, I suddenly had many of the answers I had sought desperately. But now, I was a wreck. My mind couldn't grasp the concept, and my thoughts were bouncing like a white ball in a pinball machine as I tried to reinterpret my entire life. Faced with the undeniable truth, I still couldn't understand how it was even possible. Hundreds of questions I knew I couldn't ask made a circuit through my brain.

Her eyes focused on the baby, Karis was oblivious to my turmoil and continued speaking. "Hannah is kind of a family name," she explained. My middle name is Hannah as I was named after a mysterious young woman who single-handedly rescued my entire family before I was born. They were in a bad accident and would have died if she had not gotten them out of the car and then taken them to get help. I guess there were some mysterious circumstances involved. My parents never talked about it much, except to say that it was a miracle."

"I guess I'm hoping for another miracle for my Hannah," Karis mused thoughtfully. "I don't know what we'll do if you don't think our plan will work. We've invested all of our hope in it. We won't send her if you think she won't survive or the side-effect will be too great. But, if she stays here, it's a death sentence as well. We can't know for sure what will happen if we send her back, but we know exactly what will happen if we don't. I will willingly go through the excruciating pain of giving up my daughter, if she can have a chance of a normal life. If you give your approval, then we'll just have to trust that we'll have our own Hannah-miracle on the other side of fifty-nine years."

I closed my eyes, praying that I could handle this. I was very much aware that I had fouled up previous timelines. One false move from me and I could foul this up as well. Except this time, the stakes were higher. I didn't know exactly how this episode was supposed to end, and yet I knew my very existence, my entire past and future life, was on the line.

Opening my eyes, I looked back at Karis only to see Baby Hannah batting at something shiny that was hanging around her mother's neck. It was a small heart shaped locket. *My* locket. Dad had told me it had been my mother's, but I hadn't realized at the time that the term had multiple possibilities! My own locket, an identical duplicate of the one Karis was wearing, was hidden safely under the collar of my shirt.

Seeing the locket only reinforced the pressure of how much depended on my actions in the next few minutes. I took a deep breath and tried to swallow down the emotion blocking my throat.

"Show me your research," I said finally. "You said you had tested the time machine and it works. Why is it then that you're hesitant to use it?"

"Oh, we're very confident that it works. We've done tests sending objects and mice both forward and back in small increments of time. It has been successful every time. Come here, and I will show you what the problem is."

I followed her to a shallow bin, almost like a cage, set near one of the computers. "We conducted a test yesterday where we sent a group of mice forward two minutes in time. It worked and the mice appeared to have tolerated the journey well. Now, it has been twenty-four hours since they returned."

As Karis removed the lid on the bin, I looked inside. The mice were dead.

"Every single time, we have the same results." She said with obvious frustration. "It doesn't matter if it's a shorter or a longer period of time traveled. The travelers are fine when they return. Then, twenty-four hours later, they're dead."

"Have you been able to determine the cause of death?" I

asked.

"Yes. It took a while, but we finally determined the time travel triggers the increase in the neurotransmitter tempamine. After returning, the level of tempamine increases in the brain until it becomes fatal, usually about twenty-four hours later."

That was the same reaction Seth had experienced when he had time traveled with me.

"Jason has always had more faith in this project than I." Karis continued. "He has always been sure this was the answer we needed to save our daughter. He was pretty devastated and confused when the mice died after the initial test."

"You haven't been able to find a medication or any other way to save the mice?" I asked, remembering Wayne had managed to save Seth about thirty-five years ago. Surely medicine had come far enough to get the same results.

"Oh, we can save them, but only if we administer a medication after they return. Unfortunately, that doesn't really help us with Hannah. The medication is tricky. In order to save the mice, we have to monitor them very closely. The dosage is inconsistent. Some mice might require more than others. We can't send the medication with Hannah when we send her because we won't be there to administer it. If she has trouble, no doctor from fifty-nine years ago would know how to diagnose, let alone treat her. We figure any medication we give her has to be administered before sending her. We've been trying to develop something to prevent the mice from having a chemical imbalance in the first place. Now we're out of time, and, well, you saw the results of the medicine given prior to time travel." Karis gestured to the box of dead mice.

Wayne and Seth had been trying unsuccessfully to accomplish the same goal. It certainly wasn't encouraging that my parents, who were apparently two of the most brilliant research physicians thirty-five years later, were still unable to fix the problem.

"I've been trying to use aspects of the medication that worked post-time travel as a base for the pre-time travel variety," Karis explained. "Here, I can show you the 'post-formula' I used that worked and the 'pre-formula' that obviously doesn't."

Walking back to the computer, she touched the screen, bringing up a couple of files and then projecting two chemical structures in three dimensional images side by side.

I was never more thankful for my Chemistry background. I actually understood the formulas and the ingredients that had gone into making them.

Pointing at the images, Karis explained, "I wanted to use this particular compound for the base because it brings the elevated chemical down more slowly than some other options. My theory is that if we restore the chemical balance slowly, there will be fewer side effects than a rapid change in brain chemistry. I just couldn't get the same thing to work as a preventative. I might be able to figure it out if I had more time, but we're out of that. We've had to work fast since we've only had a month to test."

After inspecting the 3-D images, I walked over to look at the computer screen.

"Feel free to look through the other files I brought up on

the computer," Karis said. "I'll be right back. This little bundle is emitting a strange odor I am hypothesizing may be toxic."

I looked at the files, detailing the ingredients, construction, and testing of both medications. There was no question. My mother was a genius. She had developed the base for the medication herself. Who knew what other uses this new medication may have?

As I analyzed the chemical recipe, it suddenly hit me. Wayne and Seth had been wrong in the direction of their research. They had been trying to prevent the chemical imbalance that caused me to time travel. Karis had been unsuccessful as well. What if they instead focused on treating my chemical imbalance *after* I time traveled? It had worked for Seth. Wayne had said that the same medication wasn't strong enough to help me, but from what I was seeing, Karis's medication might be.

I had thoroughly looked through Seth and Wayne's research, and they had done some things right. If they added Karis's base to what they had already developed, it might be enough to save my life.

Seeing that Karis was still busy changing Baby Hannah's diaper across the room, I quickly scanned the computer. If I could get a copy of this formula to Wayne and Seth, I was pretty sure they could duplicate the base. Even a computer of the future had to have a way to print. Finding the file I needed, I couldn't find the print button to save my life (literally). Karis was done. I heard her start humming a lullaby as she picked up the baby and started my way. Desperate, I was about ready to start pounding on the computer.

“Come on,” I whispered. “Please print!”

A window that read ‘Printing’ appeared on the screen. Of course! The computer was voice commanded! I gave a sigh of relief that sounded closer to a giggle as a paper fell from what was apparently a printer internal to the computer. As it landed at my feet, I swiftly picked it up.

Karis was getting closer. Seeing a pen on a nearby desk, I jotted down a few notes about adding the base to what Seth and Wayne had already developed. Writing in capital letters, I also wrote: POST-TIME TRAVEL! Dropping the pen, I quickly folded the paper up small.

I had nowhere to hide the paper--no pockets, no purse. Karis was almost behind me. Frantically, I did the first thing that popped into my head. I stuffed it down my shirt. The shirt was blousy and would hopefully hide the slight bulge. I’m not sure anyone could pull off natural and sophisticated after stuffing an object down her shirt for safekeeping, but I did my best. Turning, I met Karis with what I hoped was a serene smile.

“Honestly, Karis, your research is impeccable. I don’t have any ideas on how to make the pre-medication effective, especially on this short notice.”

Karis nodded. “I didn’t think you would.”

“But, obviously, you’re still considering sending Baby Hannah even without medication, right?”

Karis smiled sadly, “How can we think about sending her when all of our experiments have turned out so badly?’ She sighed. “Jason wanted to try it himself before sending Hannah, but I refused. He has the knowledge. If something happened to him, we would really be lost."

"Also, we can't duplicate Hannah's unique situation. Hannah is special. It is our hope that the same genetic abnormalities that would get her killed in this time, will actually protect her to journey back to another time. Neither Jason nor I have the genetic abnormalities that she has. Neither do the mice we've tested in the time machine. After extensively studying her DNA, we found she has a very strong resistance to disease and illness."

"You're the expert in human biology. This is the critical area where we need your opinion. I brought up on this second virtual screen all the research we've done on Hannah's DNA and the research on the fatal tempamine imbalance in the mice. I know you can't be 100% sure, but, in your opinion, will Hannah suffer the same tempamine imbalance as the mice, or will her unique physiology protect her?"

I obediently looked at the research on the screen that looked like a very large interactive projector. Before studying any of it, though, I already knew that the answer to Karis's question was both yes and no. Yes, Baby Hannah / I would be protected in some ways. No, I wouldn't suffer the same fate as the mice, at least not right away. But, I would still suffer a chemical imbalance that would cause consequences she would never imagine.

I was really interested in the research on Baby Hannah's / my, DNA. I had never gotten sick much growing up, and I'd always just attributed it to a little luck and a really good immune system. Now I realized it was more than that.

"I'll let you look over things, Esther. I'll be over there having some playtime with Hannah. Let me know if you need anything or have any questions."

Looking over the research, I was shocked—not as much by the actual abnormalities in my genetic code, but by the incredible advancements that had been made in the field of human genetics. The differences between my DNA and someone else's was miniscule, only a couple of slight mutations in some genes. It was shocking to realize that these mutations were detectable with routine testing and weren't considered within acceptable parameters. Genes mutated all the time! It seemed stupid and horrific that so much of the population could be labeled undesirable because of such a small thing. Apparently, in this day and age, science had progressed to the point that the goal was now the genetic engineering of humans. But, the quest for a master race, a superior human, wasn't a new one; it was just packaged in different wrapping paper.

I knew what needed to happen. I knew what I had to recommend. Baby Hannah needed to go back in time fifty-nine years. She would be healthy and raised by a loving family. She would live a happy life, at least until she was twenty-four, then the living part was still a little iffy.

I still had a hard time fathoming that my parents, Dan and Nicole Kraeger, had managed to keep everything secret my entire life. I'd never suspected that I wasn't their natural-born daughter. I still had so many questions that needed answers.

Karis had said she would be including a letter to the Kraegers with Baby Hannah. I wished there was something more I could do to ensure she would have a good reception and be raised according to my current memories. I knew my parents. They were law-abiding, rarely-think-out-of-the-box type people. This situation would be about as far out of the box as you could get. It would be a huge shock and a stretch for them to find a baby in a strange machine in their backyard. Their first inclination would be to call the authorities so they could straighten out this apparent hoax and get the baby back where she belonged. It wasn't as if I could go with the baby and make sure things were fine. My parents wouldn't even know me at that time…

Suddenly, it hit me. I *could* do something. They did know me in some way. Seeing a blank piece of paper on the desk I'd used before, I hurriedly snatched it and the pen and began writing. A couple minutes later, I was satisfied I had done everything I could to make this timeline stay true to course.

Folding the note once, I turned and walked over to where Karis was patty-caking with the baby.

"I have one question, Karis. If you send the baby back in time, what will happen to you and Jason? Won't you get in trouble when the authorities come tomorrow and find her gone?"

"We have already made preparations. If you give us the go ahead, we will send her back tonight. The minute she leaves, we will set the plan in motion to fake Hannah's death. Jason has made a very lifelike doll replica of Hannah. I will take it to another lab that has a security camera and put her in a bassinet there, as if she has just fallen asleep. A while later, I will go back to check on her only to find that she is dead. The time of death and my reaction will be on the camera as evidence."

"But won't the authorities want to see a body and know

a cause of death."

"The people coming tomorrow aren't qualified to do anything more than enforce the law. We will show them a body, the doll, and they won't check to see if it's actually real. The skin does feel like human skin, just in case, but I seriously doubt that feature will be necessary.

As for a cause of death, we have a friend who is an independent coroner. He will perform a fake autopsy and certify that Hannah's genetic abnormalities led to her death. We have also prepared fake research on her DNA that makes the abnormalities seem greater and more problematic than they actually are."

"And you think all of that will work?'

"Yes. We'll even have a memorial service for her, and, I can guarantee our grief will be genuine. By the time anyone may care to investigate, the body will have been supposedly cremated and our documentation will be in order. But, I seriously doubt we'll be investigated very thoroughly. We're important people. It is in their best interests to leave us alone and let us continue doing research. The authorities will be relieved they don't have to worry about following the law and taking Hannah away from us. It makes their job a lot easier and ensures that we can't hold a grudge against the powers that be."

It sounded as if they had thought of everything, and I was satisfied with the course of action I needed to take.

"Send her," I said with conviction. "Your research is thorough, and I believe your theory is correct. Hannah's abnormalities will protect her. She will be fine to time travel. You are saving her life. Send her."

Karis nodded, seemingly unable to speak. Her eyes were filled with a mixture of relief and intense grief.

"Thank you, Esther." She finally choked out. "I can't tell you how much…"

The loud ringing of a phone interrupted her.

Karis walked to the door and picked up a small instrument that resembled a cell phone that was mounted there.

I didn't hear the brief conversation, but I did see the dramatic change in Karis when she returned. Her eyes were wide, her face deathly pale, and she held the baby close with shaking hands.

"That was the front desk," she reported breathlessly. "Someone is here asking for us. Jason went to meet them. It's probably the authorities come to take Hannah away."

"I thought you said they weren't coming until tomorrow?"

"I did, but our contacts could have been wrong, or something may have changed. All I know is that we're not expecting anyone, and the receptionist's voice sounded very strange."

I felt my own panic rise. If they came to take Hannah now, there was no way to save her and the timeline would be destroyed. My thoughts tumbled over each other.

"Can we send her right now, Karis? Can you and I send her back in the time machine?"

"No," she said in a miserable whisper. "I don't know how to work the thing. Jason is the only one who can do it."

Karis and I stared at each other, exchanging wordless fear and helplessness. There was nothing we could do. All hope was lost. If they came for Hannah, we'd be powerless to stop them.

In less time than I thought possible, the door to the lab opened. A man in a white lab coat stepped through the door, followed by a woman. I assumed the man was Dr. Jason Blake, my father. He looked to be in his late thirties and was quite handsome. He was tall with dark wavy hair, a chiseled jaw, and piercing blue eyes. The woman was younger and very plain. She wore a brown ill-fitting suit that exactly matched the color of her bobbed brown hair. Thick rimmed glasses perched on her nose, and she was constantly pushing them back up into place, whether they needed it or not.

"Jason?" Karis questioned hesitantly.

"Karis, this is Dr. Esther Jefferies," he said, nodding toward the woman beside him."

"But,... that can't be," Karis replied, confused. Motioning to me, she insisted, "This is Esther Jefferies."

"I checked her ID, Karis." Jason explained, shooting confused, nervous glances my way. "Dr. Jefferies is late because she was given the wrong directions. She's been wandering around the Jackson area for a couple of hours."

The petite woman spoke up indignantly, "I don't know who this other woman is, but she is definitely not *me*."

"But, I thought..." Karis turned her gaze on me, her expression suddenly changing from confused and vulnerable to very angry. Cuddling Baby Hannah close, she became a mother bear, interpreting me as a threat to her child. "You just told me to put my daughter in that machine! You looked at all of our research and said she would be safe. How dare you? Who exactly are you? Were you sent to check up on us? I told you everything!"

Jason put his arm around Karis. His eyes stared at me with a look I couldn't define, almost as if he was pleading for something.

Hating to see the tears streaming down my mother's face and the fearful confusion lining my father's, I hurried to explain as best I could. "You're right. I'm not Esther Jefferies. But, I haven't come to harm your baby in any way. I only want to help." Holding the folded paper out like a white flag, I made Jason take it, saying, "Here, take this letter and put it with Hannah when you send her back in time. You probably shouldn't read it though. It would only confuse matters. You'll have to trust me, I guess."

"Trust you? How can we trust you?" Karis protested, almost sputtering at my audacity. "You deceived me!"

"I still think you should send her. It's the only way to save her. She will be fine, I know it. You *must* send her."

"You know? How do you know she'll be fine? You're obviously not the expert we thought you were." Karis argued. "You saw our research, but what qualifies you to make a recommendation like that?"

With one forceful, almost desperate question, Jason got to the heart of the matter. "WHO ARE YOU?"

I bit my lip in indecision. My parents were still looking at me with masks of anger, confusion, and fear on their faces. I didn't know what to do. Feeling helpless, I looked at the baby in Karis's arms. Oblivious to the life and death drama going on around her, she was happily grabbing at her mother's shiny gold necklace.

Suddenly, I had an idea. There was only one way to make them understand, one way to make them follow through with their plan of sending Baby Hannah back in time, one way to save the timeline and my own life.

Reaching into the collar of my blouse, I felt the delicate chain around my neck and pulled out the tiny heart locket, identical to the one Karis was wearing around her neck. Holding it with shaking fingers for them to see, I looked into their eyes and begged them to understand. With a whisper that echoed in the silent room, I confessed, "I am Hannah."

Anxiously studying their faces, I tried to read their reactions. Jason looked uncertain and confused, as if his brain wasn't processing this new information fast enough. Focusing on Karis's face, I saw incredible shock. She looked at me, then down at her baby's face, then back at me. Understanding dawned like a brilliant sun making its morning debut over a mountain range. Tears filled her eyes, but they couldn't drown the sudden love and excitement that shone from their blue depths.

Seeing that she understood, I felt a sudden peace pour over me. Tears burned the back of my eyes and slid down my face as I tried to hold back the sobs of pure relief.

She believed me!

She would now send Baby Hannah back fifty-nine years to be raised by a family she'd never met.

My body felt weak with the sudden release of tension. My legs felt like wet noodles and my breathing excited and irregular. I wasn't sure I could continue standing.

This was my mother!

As I looked into her eyes, it was as if everything in my life suddenly fell into place. Everything was as it should be.

My mother, still holding Baby Hannah, reached out her shaking hand for my own. I stretched my own hand to meet hers, but our skin never touched. Like someone had dumped a bucket of water over a beautiful painting, the images of my parents dissolved before my eyes. In the time it took to blink once, the colors came back together into a new, familiar painting. A tire swing hung from a large tree. I was home.

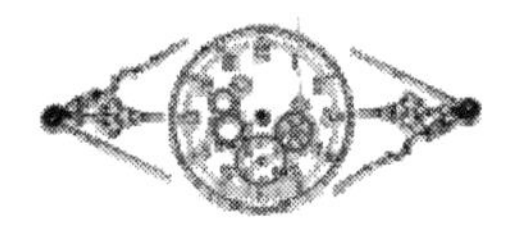

CHAPTER NINE

I didn't wait for my vision to clear. I didn't wait for the pain and dizziness to hit. I knew I didn't have time. Recognizing where I was, I turned and started running, yelling, and pulling at my blouse all at the same time.

"Help!" I screamed at the top of my lungs. "Help! I'm here! I'm here!"

I didn't make it to the back door of the house. I don't think I made it ten steps before the pain hit. Feeling like that stupid fire truck had come back and hit me, I suddenly found myself on the ground not knowing which end was up. I finally managed to get the paper untangled from my blouse, clasping my hand in a vise around it.

I tried to stand back up and couldn't make my body obey. Pain and nausea threatened to overwhelm me. I felt the blackness calling to me, grabbing at me and trying to pull me down into its depths. I couldn't give in to it. I knew I may never wake if I did.

Willing my mind to not slip into unconsciousness, I began crawling toward the back door. I had to make it. I had to get help.

Suddenly, the glass door slid open.

"She's here!" Seth yelled, running to my side. "I found her! She's here."

Bending over me, I saw the stark fear in Seth's eyes right before he slipped into doctor mode and began trying to assess my condition.

"Seth,…" I whispered.

"It's okay, Hannah. You're going to be fine."

He felt my pulse, looked in my eyes, and seemed to be looking me over for any injury. The pain was so intense, I wanted to scream. It felt as if my head was splitting open. I knew this may be the last time I ever saw Seth's face, but I couldn't make the colors stop swirling in nauseating patterns.

"Seth, wait!" I protested weakly as he started to lift me.

"I need to get you inside, Hannah. Wayne's here. We've been waiting for you. We'll try whatever we can. I'm not going to lose you." His doctor façade was cracking. His voice shook with emotion, and I could tell that deep down, he had no idea how to save my life.

I tried to speak, to explain what I had discovered, but I couldn't form words anymore. Weakly, I raised my hand and pressed the paper into his. I didn't know if he took the paper or if my action registered with him. The blackness had overtaken me, and I knew nothing.

During the previous times I'd recovered from time travel, I had liked the blackness. It had been a comforting shelter where I could hide from excruciating pain. That same blackness that I had so welcomed before, I now fought with everything that was in me. It was evil. It wrapped around me like ropes and held me down in a deep ocean. I felt as if I was drowning. I struggled, trying to claw my way to the surface.

For brief snatches of reality, I would surface to consciousness. I'd hear voices around me. At one point, I woke enough to hear the arguing voices of Seth and Wayne.

"How close are you, Wayne?" I heard Seth ask.

"I'm not sure. This isn't exactly easy, and without time to test it to make sure I got it right…"

"Come on, Wayne! You had the formula. You said you could do it."

"I don't see you helping, Seth!"

"You told me not to! You said to get out of the way! You're better at formulas than I am. I've been monitoring Hannah. You said you could do it!"

"I can! I will!"

"She's dying, Wayne!" Seth exploded. "Time's up! It may be too late. Her vitals are getting more erratic. She's fighting, but I don't know how much more she can take. She's losing."

"You're not telling me anything I don't already know,

Seth! Don't make the mistake of thinking that you're the only one in this room who cares about her! I'll get it done. I'm almost there."

The blackness pulled me down again, and after that, it was increasingly difficult to make it to the surface. Seth had been right. I was losing the battle. The darkness was becoming thicker, and it was harder to breathe. It was deceptive, again promising warmth and comfort if I would just let it take me where it wanted. I was dying.

Knowing I had to at least tell Seth goodbye, I put all of my strength into fighting to consciousness one last time. I became aware of someone holding my hand, of wet drops falling on the back side of that hand, and of the sound of someone sobbing quietly.

"Seth," I whispered, reaching out that wet hand until it connected with the rough skin of my beloved's face.

"I'm sorry," I whispered, not knowing if I was actually managing to get sound out and if he was actually hearing it. "So very sorry."

"No, Hannah, please," he begged. "Don't give up. Keep fighting. Don't leave me."

I tried. The darkness grabbed me and mercilessly pulled me down. I was so very tired. I imagined this was kind of like freezing to death. One would just fall asleep and die. I wasn't ready to die, though. I wanted to live.

All of the events leading to this moment in my life had been too bizarre and complicated to be random. Deep down, I still felt that my steps were ordered by a higher power. I knew Him. If God had truly gone to so much trouble to save me, I couldn't imagine He was done with me yet. With everything that had happened, I felt that if I was to die now, my life would be an incomplete sentence.

I concentrated on not thinking beyond the next breath. In and out. Just one more. I kept telling myself that I could rest after this next breath. Again and again, until finally, something changed.

It was easier to breathe, and the darkness didn't seem so sinister. I could relax without being afraid that it would drag me down further. At last, I did sleep.

I came awake suddenly. One second I was unaware; the next, I opened my eyes and noticed Seth's vicious black eye. I figured I must be alive because I didn't think anyone in heaven would have that kind of shiner.

"Who did you fight with?" I asked, without preamble.

Seth looked up and grinned widely. "Well, hello, to you too, Beautiful!"

"Who did you fight with?" I repeated.

Seth grimaced and touched what had to be a very painful injury.

"Wayne," he finally admitted.

And Wayne chose that exact second to enter the room. Seeing the two of them standing side by side, I burst into laughter, not really caring that my guffaws weren't doing the pain in my head any favors. These two, highly intelligent, prominent doctors, had matching black eyes.

The men looked at each other, then back at me.

"So glad we could amuse you, Hannah," Wayne said,

touching his own injury with a grimace."

"Why the fight?" I asked finally, the pain in my head demanding my enjoyment stop for the moment.

"You." Wayne answered flatly. Seeing my shocked, confused look, he continued. "Let's just say, Seth didn't respond well when you disappeared, he couldn't reach you by cell phone. I had to tell him what you and I had discussed over donuts."

I turned accusing eyes Seth's direction. "Don't look at me that way!" he protested. "It's not like Wayne was passive in our… discussion. He gave as good as he got, obviously."

I saw Wayne's smile as Seth gestured to his injured eye.

"Here's my question," Seth continued, coming closer to me. "You run off despite my wishes, time travel who knows where, return with some miracle formula, almost die, and the first thing you want to know is how we got matching black eyes? Come on, Hannah."

"So all of that wasn't a dream," I said, suddenly weary.

"To quote a wise television character who was involved with a very disobedient woman, Hannah, 'you've got some explaining to do,'" Wayne chimed in, using a pretty lousy Desi Arnez impersonation.

I recognized the quote from "I Love Lucy," and rolled my eyes. As I did, my current location finally registered. I wasn't in a hospital. I was in my own room at my parent's house in Jackson. The frilly blue curtains hung in the window. My artwork graced the walls in both murals and frames. The ceiling itself was painted as a mural of the sky with fluffy white clouds parading across. I was in my own comfy, four poster bed I had received for my sixteenth birthday.

"Why am I not in a hospital?" I asked curiously.

"We thought it would be safer to keep you here," Seth explained. "While I was still on my way here to try to stop you, your parents called me wondering where you were. They said your SUV was in the driveway, but they couldn't find you anywhere. I knew then that you had time traveled. I called Wayne, and he put together all of the medical equipment we might need and met me here."

Wayne took over the explanation. "We knew when you returned, we wouldn't be able to admit you back into the hospital with the same mysterious symptoms. There would have been too many questions and too much to explain. No matter what condition you returned in, we knew we'd have to treat you here."

Nodding, Seth said, "Wayne had been hoping to try to make some last minute adjustments on his medication for you. Fortunately, he brought everything he needed to make the new compound outlined on that paper you gave me. If he hadn't already had the supplies, I don't think you would have made it. Right now, it's only been twenty-four hours since you returned."

"About that formula, Hannah," Wayne said. "Where did you get it? I've never seen anything like it. I certainly don't think I could have ever come up with a base like that. It took me a while to figure it out and make it on such short notice, but it's pure genius."

"Maybe we should ask *when* you got it, Hannah." Seth

chimed in. "When you disappeared, I had to fill your parents in on everything."

Seth must have seen my eyes widening as immediate questions filled my mind.

He held up his hands to stop the torrent. "Wait, Hannah, let me finish. I know nothing. They wouldn't tell me anything. They know something, but all they would say was that they'd have to discuss it with you when you returned."

Wayne filled in, "All of us, including your parents, tried to figure out what time you may have gone to. We racked our brains for any other memories or encounters with you in our past. None of us could come up with anything new."

"So, Hannah," Seth asked, "you went back in time to when?"

"Well, I don't think 'back in time' is really the correct term in this instance."

Both men's eyes widened in shock.

"The future?" Seth whispered.

I nodded. They both opened their mouths to unleash their interrogation. I held up my hand to stop them. "My parents, Seth, I need to see my parents. You'll understand things better if they're here."

Seth suddenly lost all of his bedside manner. "Absolutely not, Hannah. The last time you tried to talk to them, you didn't even make it in the door before your emotions sent you on a trip apparently to the future. You've only been back twenty-four hours. In that span of time, you almost died! There's no way we're going to risk a repeat."

"You don't have to worry about that." I argued. "Talking to them isn't going to trigger me time traveling."

"You've said that before," Seth grumbled.

"But this time, I already know the answers. I know the circumstances of my birth. I even know why I time travel. I just need to hear their side of it to fill in the holes. Unless another diabolical fire engine comes by, I should be fine."

"Well, if you already know everything, why don't you fill us in?" Seth urged.

"No, I really need to talk to them first. It'll make a lot more sense, I think, if you hear their side of it as well."

Both Seth and Wayne still looked skeptical. Seth still looked like I might be able to see my parents over his dead body.

"How are you feeling, Hannah?" Wayne asked.

I didn't answer, angry at the obvious subject change.

Seth sighed. "It's been only about three hours since you came very close to dying, Hannah. Your breathing was erratic and every heartbeat I feared may be your last. Wayne finished the medication, we administered it, and now you are awake and talking. At the time, we didn't know if it would work. So, now we need to know, how do you feel?"

"Of course it worked. Have you been testing my levels? The formula for the compound I gave you gradually decreases the elevated tempamine. Wayne, you had mentioned something before about it being the rapid fall was what was hard for my body to recover from. Slow that down and bingo, Hannah is alive."

Seth and Wayne looked at each other, obviously impressed and slightly confused by my understanding.

"Hannah, you're about to drive me crazy," Seth moaned. "I don't really care how the medication works, what I want to know is, HOW DO YOU FEEL?"

"Like crap!" I snapped cantankerously. "I have a splitting headache, dizziness, and nausea. But compared to how I felt when I was dying, I feel wonderful!

"See, was that too hard?" Seth asked, glaring, but with a sparkle in his eyes. Wayne was chuckling outright as he worked on something over by the desk.

"Now that we have that cleared up," I said, returning his glare, "let's get back to the subject. I'm not asking your permission, Seth. Either you two get my parents up here, or I'm going to crawl out of this bed and go find them myself."

"Okay, Hannah," Seth conceded. "You win."

"I'll run down and get them myself," Wayne volunteered. "Right after your medicine."

A sudden, ornery smile creased Seth's face.

"We actually have been monitoring your levels, Hannah," Wayne said, walking toward me with a wicked looking syringe. "And by my calculations, you are due for another dose."

"Why do I get the feeling this is going to be an embarrassing and highly humiliating experience?"

"We're professionals, Hannah," Wayne assured. "And this isn't your first dose."

"It shouldn't be humiliating at all, Sweetheart," Seth

chimed in, using a calming voice. "You have a very nice bare bottom."

The evil man! My face flamed red, as I'm sure he knew it would. I turned on my side and buried my face in my pillow. Before I knew what was happening, Wayne had given me the injection. To my relief, the target had actually been my hip more than my "very nice bare bottom."

My head still buried in its white cocoon, I heard the door open and close as Wayne left the room on his errand. I felt the mattress sag as Seth lay on the edge of the bed beside me and pulled me in his arms.

"Look at me, my Hannah," he whispered. "I like you in red."

He gently touched my cheek with the back of his hand. "Don't worry. We're going to work on getting your medication into pill form as soon as we can. We just didn't have time."

"How long will I have to take it?" I asked.

"I don't know. We've been monitoring your levels closely and will have to continue doing so. But, as you know, a lot of this is guesswork. It appears that the medication has dramatically slowed the tempamine decline. The downside is that it's going to take a lot longer for your levels to get back into proper balance. It might be two weeks or longer. During this time, you may be more susceptible to time travel because you're already at an imbalance."

I nodded and closed my eyes. It felt so good to feel Seth's arm around me, to feel the touch of his hand, to smell the musky scent that always surrounded him.

"The tempmine had already dropped significantly before we were able to give you the medicine. You were in such bad shape, we were afraid it was going to be too little too late. I was so scared. I thought we were going to lose you."

Seth's eyes looked shiny, as if he was trying to fight back tears. As he talked, I gently reached up and caressed the tender skin under his eye. "I can't put into words how much I love you. Without you I feel incomplete. I live to see your smile. I look into your eyes and find the missing puzzle piece in my life. It's like you're a vital part of me, necessary to my existence. I can't imagine life without my Hannah"

"I'm so sorry I put you through all that, Seth," I responded, biting my lip and turning my eyes from the raw emotion in Seth's eyes. "I should have listened to you. I was stupid. I thought I could handle my emotions. Obviously, I couldn't. Being startled by a stupid fire truck was enough to send me over the edge and years into the future. When I realized what had happened, I thought I was going to die. I hated what I had done to you and couldn't handle the thought of not being with you. You are the reason I'm still here. You're the reason I fought so hard."

Seth brought my hand up to his lips and kissed it tenderly. "I'm sorry too, Hannah. I know I have been really distant lately. I've been so afraid of doing something that might take you away. I've treated you like fragile china. I've been afraid to kiss you, touch you, or even tell you how I feel. I should have done better. Maybe if I would have listened to your concerns and answered your questions, you wouldn't have tried to do things on your own. If I could've been there with you to talk to your parents, maybe this wouldn't have happened."

"Don't play the 'if only' game, Seth. Everything worked out. I found my answers and was able to come back with a way to save my life. I think we were very fortunate this time."

Unspoken between us was the knowledge that the new medication would do nothing to prevent me from time traveling again. A lot of the issues still remained. I could be ripped back out of Seth's reach at any time.

Seth cuddled me close as if he was afraid to let me go for even a second. He smoothed my hair away from my face and trailed tender kisses on my brow. A knock sounded at the door. Seth sighed, quickly released me and stood before the door opened.

My mom rushed into the room, tears streaming down her face. "Oh, Hannah, you're awake! I was so scared. I wanted to stay with you, but these two brutes wouldn't let me. They said I couldn't be here when you woke up. I've been pacing the floor downstairs and seriously considering finding a ladder to climb through your window."

I smiled, trying to imagine my petite, ladylike mom climbing through a window and taking out two young doctors. My dad was standing behind Mom, looking at me with both relief and a cautious curiosity.

Meeting his eyes, I said, "Hi, Dad. It seems like only a few months ago I was putting Baby Abby into your arms for the first time. Although it seems to me you had quite a bit more hair back then."

Dad suddenly grinned, "And you, my dear, don't look like you've aged a day in twenty-six years. In fact, you don't look a day over twenty-four yourself."

Everyone paused, waiting. My parents obviously knew Seth and I had delivered Abby and saved Mom, but they seemed to be waiting for me to explain exactly how much I knew.

Trying to figure out where to start, I finally just dove in. "Yesterday I traveled about thirty-five years in the future. I met my biological parents, Jason and Karis Blake."

The room was completely silent for about ten solid seconds.

As if something just occurred to him, Seth broke the silence. "Wait. Isn't the Lawson's baby named Karis?" Seth asked.

"Yes, my biological mother is currently a one-year-old toddler named Karis Lawson. When she grows up, she will become a brilliant research doctor and marry another doctor and engineer named Jason Blake. A little less than thirty-five years from now, they will have a baby girl named Hannah—me."

Seth had turned pale as I spoke, and, as if he were unsteady on his feet, he suddenly sat down in the chair by my desk. Wayne, having an incurable fascination with the bizarre, had a huge grin on his face. My parents didn't look shocked at all. They just nodded their heads.

"We didn't know all of the details," Dad explained. "But, putting two and two together, we kind of suspected you might have been born in the future. It isn't every day somebody finds a baby in a strange machine in their back yard."

"Why didn't you ever tell me I wasn't your biological daughter?" I asked. "You could have at least said I was adopted."

"You told us not to!" Dad said.

Mom walked over to my dresser and picked up a piece of paper that was covered in plastic. Returning to my bed, she handed it to me. "I've kept this away from the other things ever since I realized you were the one who wrote it. I was looking at it again this morning, hoping it might give us some clue as to how to help you."

The letter she handed me was obviously old, twenty-four years old by this timeline. Mom had tried to protect the letter, encasing it in a clear plastic covering. Though now yellowed and brittle, this was the same piece of paper I'd held in my parent's lab. Recognizing my own handwriting, I reread the words I had so hurriedly written only yesterday.

Dear Mr. Kraeger,

Two years ago I and my doctor friend were in the right place at the right time to save the lives of your wife and daughter. When I put Abby in your arms, you asked me if there was any way you could ever repay me. Now, you are in the right place at the right time to save the life of this baby. Consider this your repayment. Consider her your daughter. Rest assured there is nothing untoward or illegal in taking her as your own. There are unusual circumstances involved, as there were unusual circumstances two years ago. Follow the instructions given to you precisely, but do not mention to Hannah the strange events surrounding her joining your family until she asks you about them directly. Above all, love her.

Sincerely,

A Friend

Tears blurred my vision. My parents had followed my instructions to the letter.

"Thank you, Mom and Dad," I said, my voice too choked up to speak above a whisper. "Thank you… for everything."

"Oh, Hannah," Mom replied, choked up as well. "We've been the ones who've been blessed by you. We should be thanking you for everything."

Seth had crowded beside me and read over my shoulder. Finishing, he looked at me in confusion. "I don't understand. You wrote this letter, Hannah?"

Obviously curious about our strange conversation, Wayne was not willing to be left out. He came to the other side of my bed, took the letter and read it as well.

"Yes, I wrote it yesterday, which for all intent and purposes was thirty-five years in the future. Then, I gave it to Jason and Karis to send back fifty-nine years to the Kraegers. I assume Mom and Dad received it when they found me in the backyard twenty-four years ago."

"I'm still confused," Seth protested. "Why and how did Jason and Karis send Baby You and the letter back in time to Dan and Nicole?"

I figured the best shot at Seth understanding was to start at the beginning and give a brief summary of my experience. "Yesterday, I met Dr. Karis Blake at a research facility where she worked. She assumed I was the colleague she sent for to get a second opinion. I, of course, had no idea who she was or her connection to me. Through her explanation and our conversation, I found that her baby girl was going to be taken away from them because she had some genetic abnormalities. These abnormalities were in no way detrimental to her health, but the authorities were very intolerant of what they felt was imperfect DNA."

"To save their daughter, Jason had developed a time machine to send her back to a time where she would be safe. They had researched and found that a wonderful family by the name of Kraeger had once lived in the exact location of their current research facility. Their plan was to save their daughter by giving her to the Kraegers. They even had completed adoption papers valid for the time frame the Kraegers were living in."

"The only problem was that their preliminary experiments with sending mice in the time machine resulted in death. Karis had developed a formula that could save the mice after they time traveled, but she had run out of time to modify it for a necessary pre-travel medication. Their hope, however, was that medication would be unnecessary and their daughter's genetic abnormalities would protect her."

"Of course, I knew Baby Me, would be fine for the journey. Even though they discovered I wasn't their colleague, I was still able to convince them to send their daughter. I wrote the letter hoping that it would help the

Kraegers accept the baby and raise me in the wonderful way I remembered."

Picking up the story where I left off, Dad took over, "Twenty-four years ago yesterday, we heard a strange noise in our backyard. We went outside to find a large bizarre-looking machine. As we watched, a door opened automatically, and we heard a baby crying. We discovered your letter along with other letters, instructions, and paperwork from your parents. After reading everything, we decided the only thing we could do was follow the instructions exactly. Besides that, your mother and I fell in love with you the very first time we saw you. It felt as if you were always meant to be our daughter."

Mom chimed in, "Until you told us just now, we never knew any of the details of why you were sent to us. We were terrified at first. We were afraid people would ask questions or you might be taken away from us. But, amazingly, no one ever asked to see your adoption papers. Everyone took our word that you were legally ours. We had to show your birth certificate a few times, like when you entered school, but your parents actually sent two versions, one listing them as biological parents and one listing us as biological parents. We chose to use the second one, and no one ever asked about it."

"I understand why you didn't tell me," I said. "But, you've lived in the same town my entire life. Other people had to have known I was adopted, right?"

"Yes, they did," Mom said. "We initially made no secret that we had adopted you. Everyone was overjoyed for us. After a while, though, it's almost as if people forgot. Everyone began to say how much you and Abby looked alike. People assumed you were biological sisters. We told Grandma and the rest of the family that there were some unusual circumstances surrounding your adoption. We said we'd been advised, for your safety, to not widely publicize or tell you about the adoption until you were older. They already loved you like their own and took what we said at face value. It still is kind of amazing to me that everything went so smoothly. It really is a miracle in a lot of ways."

"So, you didn't know I was actually born in the future?" I asked.

"No. We had our suspicions though. One of your dad's initial crazy theories had been that the contraption was a time machine. When all of these strange things started happening to you around Christmastime, we were pretty sure your history had something to do with time travel, but, because both you and your parents warned us in your letters, we couldn't discuss it with you until now."

"But, you had to have realized before Christmas that I was the person who helped deliver Abby and then wrote that letter."

Dad cleared his throat. "About the time you turned sixteen, I looked at you one day and realized you looked very similar to the young woman who had delivered Abby. I mentioned it to your mom, but I couldn't be for sure. We knew there had been some unusual circumstances surrounding that incident. We had found that there was never any record or picture of a Dr. McAllister or his nurse at the hospital. It about drove the doctor who had shown up late insane. He didn't understand how two people could so thoroughly disappear. But, I also knew I had been extremely emotional at that time and couldn't really trust my memory."

"It wasn't until Christmas, when we met your Dr. Seth McAllister for the first time, that I knew for sure it had been you. The two of you seemed to have no memory of those events surrounding Abby's birth, so we felt it wise to keep quiet until we had some kind of signal from you."

Wayne had been quiet, but now he spoke up with his own question. "What happened to the time machine Hannah arrived in?"

Dad answered, "We saved all of the things that arrived with Hannah, but we destroyed the actual machine. Included with Hannah's papers were detailed instructions on how to dismantle and damage it beyond repair. It was made very clear that the machine was dangerous and could not be used or seen by anyone else. I didn't know what it was, but I followed the instructions to the letter, even burning flammable parts and taking pieces to several different dumps."

Wayne looked like a little boy who'd had his new Christmas toy taken away. Suddenly, he brightened, and eagerly picked up my hand, holding it gently in his own.

Seeing Wayne's action, I could feel the sudden tension from Seth on my other side. Glancing at his face, I saw that he was glaring at Wayne and practically growling.

"What?" Wayne asked Seth innocently. "I figured that with Hannah's time machine destroyed, the only hope I ever have of time traveling is Hannah herself."

Looking at me with wide, pleading, puppy dog eyes, Wayne continued, "Hannah, next time you go back to the future, will you please, please, please take me with you?"

I jerked my hand away from his. With one swift motion,

I grabbed the pillow from behind me and threw it at his silly grin.

Everybody in the room was laughing, feeling the release of tension from the past twenty-four hours and the relief that everything was now out in the open. I, on the other hand, didn't find Wayne's request the least bit funny.

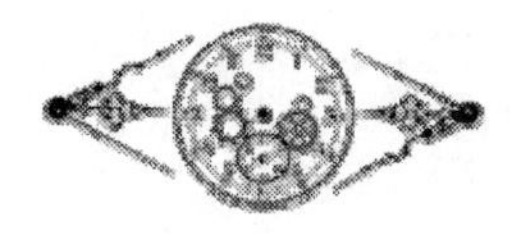

CHAPTER TEN

I heard the doorbell ring downstairs. I wasn't expecting Mom and Abby until a little later. I started to run downstairs to answer it, but at the top of the stairs, I heard Natalie open the door and greet someone. Maybe she was expecting company. After all, it was her house.

I turned back to my room to put the finishing touches on my hair. It had been a full two weeks since my trip to the future, but I was still feeling a little weak. Seth thought it was probably because the medication reduced the imbalance so slowly that I was still having a few side effects. Overall, though, I couldn't complain. I would take a little fatigue and weakness over the alternative any day.

A couple minutes later, I heard Natalie calling my name. Maybe it was Mom or Abby who'd been at the door after all. We were all supposed to have a girls' night tonight. An evening of dinner and watching chick flicks may not sound like much, but I was looking forward to it.

Reaching the bottom of the stairs, I saw Wayne talking to Natalie.

"Dr. Hawkins will see you now, Hannah," Natalie announced playfully. "I'm going to get to work on those brownies to go with our ice cream and hot fudge tonight."

Natalie was somewhat of a mystery to me. She wasn't nosy at all. She was not an eavesdropper and never seemed curious about other's personal business. She was interested in anything I told her, but she never probed for more information. She accepted at face value whatever I told her.

I was her roommate, yet she still knew nothing about my time traveling. On some level, she had to know there was something strange going on with me. She knew Seth had looked for me for years, she knew there were unusual circumstances when we first met and I saved Wayne from sacrificing himself for Katherine, she also knew that I'd had some strange health problems recently. But, she never asked about it.

It was almost as if she didn't want to know. A couple of times, she'd been in the room when Seth or Wayne stopped by to see how I was feeling. She would immediately leave or become busy doing something else. It wasn't as if she didn't care; she was always doing nice things, checking on me, and in general being a wonderful friend. Maybe it was because she knew something freaky was going on with me that she just didn't want to know the reality of it.

As Natalie made her quick exit, I plopped on the couch across from Wayne.

"I didn't expect to see you today, Wayne. Seth had said you guys were slammed with work."

"We are. Seth is especially busy with working on his anti-depressant research. With the official opening of our facility coming up, we have a lot of details to take care of."

"I wish I could help you guys," I said.

My relationships with Seth and my family had been a lot better the past two weeks. They had all realized that trying to protect and shield me from stressful emotions and situations was doing more harm than good. Everything was a lot more natural now. Seth was open and loving. He took time out of his busy schedule practically every day to talk and spend time with me.

The only thing he absolutely would not let me do yet was go back to work. He said their research start-up was really stressful at the moment because of their preparations with their investor for the official opening. He didn't want me near that level of stress yet. No matter what we did, the fear I would disappear into another time was always lurking in the background. So, much to my annoyance, I was currently unemployed.

"Well, maybe you can come back to rescue us sooner than you think," Wayne said, an excited light in his eyes. "I'm here with news. Seth wanted to come with me to tell you, but he had a meeting and then some important errands he had to run this evening."

"I'm listening," I said, leaning forward on the couch.

"I remember you saying that your biological mother, Karis Blake, had been working on a medication to administer pre-time travel that would prevent the tempamine imbalance."

"Yes, she had developed the formula that would work post-time travel, the same one I gave to you for my medication. She was trying to use that same formula as a base for the new medication, but she ran out of time. She seemed to think she could figure it out if she didn't have such a deadline, but I don't know. I think she probably ran into some of the same problems with making a before-medication that you did."

"Not exactly," Wayne said. "I was intrigued by your mother's formula and also by the fact that she thought she could be successful with a before-medication. Seth and I have been working on it since then, and we think we've done it! It wasn't nearly as difficult as I would've thought. As I've said before, your mom's formula is genius. I could've never figured it out without it, but with it, it was a relatively easy, though time-consuming process."

I was surprised and touched. I knew how busy they had been with their own workloads, and now I found they had been spending considerable time working on my problem.

"Are you saying that you've developed something I can take to prevent tempamine in my brain from spiking and triggering time travel?" I asked, wanting to make sure I fully understood.

"Yes, Hannah, I believe so."

Tears flooded my eyes. "I had no idea you were working on that. I don't know what to say. Thank you seems inadequate."

Wayne seemed to brush off my emotion as he handed me a small plastic medicine bottle and leapt into an explanation.

"You'll have to take a pill every day. You can start today if you want to. The theory is that if we have a steady level of this medication in you, it will prevent the spikes tempamine makes with your emotions. It uses the same base formula that we gave you after you returned, but it's tweaked a little and at a much lower dose."

I opened the cap on the medicine bottle and looked at the tiny white pills inside. Although I didn't like the idea of having to take a pill every day for the rest of my life, it would be well worth it. I knew this was the best thing for me, but, as I removed one pill and held it in my hand, I couldn't stem the wave of discouragement flooding over me. Taking the pill almost felt like a defeat instead of the victory of solving my problem. Deep down, I guess I'd been hoping the problem would go away as suddenly and magically as it appeared.

"Part of me is still confused about why this is an issue for me in the first place," I said, admitting some of my feelings to Wayne. "I understand my genetic abnormalities probably protected me when I was initially sent in the time machine. The mice died, I lived. What I don't understand is if that initial time travel messed me up and causes me to travel on my own now, why was it not a problem for the first twenty-three years of my life? It doesn't make sense that last Christmas was the first time I had supposed side effects from an event that took place twenty-three years ago."

"I wish I had a definite answer for you, Hannah, but I don't. Seth and I have talked about it, but the only explanation we reached was that the onset of your tempamine imbalance was similar to the onset of some migraines. Some people, women especially, who have never had migraines can suddenly start suffering from serious debilitating migraines in their early twenties. The theory is that something changes in the brain as it reaches that point in maturity. Your brain chemistry could have changed as well, triggering the potential for a chemical imbalance, the roots of which lay with traveling in a time machine as a baby."

In the end, I realized that it didn't really matter how the problem started. If I faced reality, it didn't seem to be going away. In a sense, I chose it. I knew the difficulties I would face if Jason and Karis sent their baby back in time, and I told them to do it anyway. Now, with a tiny white pill, Wayne was offering me a chance at a normal life once again—a life I would have never had as Jason and Karis's daughter.

Reaching for the glass of water I had left on the coffee table earlier, I quickly swallowed my first pill.

Wayne smiled. "Now that we got that taken care of, I have a question for you. I've been curious about what happened when you were in the future."

I looked at Wayne cautiously. "I didn't hear who won the World Series, if that's what you're asking."

He laughed. "No, but I would appreciate any subtle hints along those lines. Actually, I was wondering about how you got the paper you gave Seth. You know, the one that had the formula and the instructions for how to integrate it with the work we'd already done. I know the formula was Karis Blake's, but she couldn't have known about our work. She couldn't have known how to mesh the two together."

I smiled a little sheepishly, "Well, I may have understood a little more about your research than I led you to believe. What can I say? I'm good at Chemistry, Wayne. I analyzed your research, knew the problems you were running into, and the current medication you were working on. When I saw Karis's medication for the mice, I didn't think it would work for me because we couldn't reproduce it. It had several elements I didn't recognize. The base formula, however, was what she was trying to use in her further research. I thought it would work with what you had already done. I printed out Karis's formula without her seeing, wrote the brief instructions about what to do, and then hid the paper on my person so that it would travel back with me whenever I went."

Wayne looked impressed. "I knew you were smart, Hannah, but you just have a minor in Chemistry, right? The understanding you're talking about is well beyond that. You're saying you just looked at it and knew how the medication should be constructed? Hannah, you're not good at Chemistry, you're gifted!"

I made a face. "Now you sound like my Chemistry professors."

"Seth mentioned a while back that you had talked about going back to get some kind of degree in Chemistry. Are you still thinking about it? Have the classes started yet?"

"Classes for the fall semester start at the end of next month. I've already taken the entrance exams and been accepted to the program. They'll let me go directly into the graduate program and work on my Masters degree."

Wayne looked excited and leaned forward in his chair, grabbing my hand in his. "Hannah, you have to do it. You have a gift, and it would be a crime not to use it. From what you've told me, your parents will be outstanding in the field of medicine, and they've obviously passed their talent down to you. We could really use your help with our research company. Seth and I tend to get so focused sometimes that we can't see the forest for the trees. We really need the fresh opinion of someone who really understands what we're doing."

"I'll think about it, Wayne."

"Don't think about it, Hannah, do it. You can still do your art, but this is your chance to really help others. The kind of work we'll be doing helps people by changing and saving lives."

"I'll think about it," I repeated, more sternly this time. Looking into my eyes for a long moment, as if trying to assess how serious I was, Wayne finally sighed, released my hand, and stood.

"I've got to go. I have a meeting in Suasilito this evening, and I have to get some work done before that."

Standing with him, I impulsively wrapped my arms around him in a hug, and stood on my tiptoes to plant a kiss on his cheek.

"Thank you, Wayne," I said softly. "Thank you for saving my life two weeks ago and for giving me the hope of a normal life now. I think you have more than repaid anything I ever did for you."

Wayne looked surprised and a little unnerved by my show of affection.

He gently lifted my chin with his hand so my eyes met his serious chocolate brown ones. "It's not the same thing, Hannah. In a lot of ways, you saved your own life. You were the one who got the formula and figured out how to integrate it with the work I'd already done. What you did for me several years ago still affects everything about my life today. The connection I feel to you hasn't gone away because I was able to help you. I don't think I'll ever be free of you." His fingers gently caressed down my cheek, and I couldn't look away from the emotion in his eyes. He finally whispered, "I don't think I want to be."

Dropping his hand suddenly, he blinked and looked away.

In a normal tone, like he'd been discussing the weather, Wayne said, "It would probably be best if you took the medication at the same time every day, Hannah. Don't forget. And tell Natalie that she's going to owe me one of those brownies next time I see her. They actually smell better than my brownies, and that's saying something."

Had I just imagined an emotional moment with Wayne? He snapped out of it so suddenly, I wondered if it had happened. As he went out the door with a cheerful wave, I shrugged off a slightly unsettled feeling and instead felt so thankful that Wayne was in my life.

From that experience over three and a half years ago, Wayne and I had developed a deep connection of friendship. It was nice to know someone cared about me as much as he did. My relationship with Wayne was what I imagined it would feel like to have an older brother. He would always be there to love me, protect me, and fight my battles if need be. Unlike a lot of friendships, I didn't feel like I had to be or act a certain way with Wayne, I only felt acceptance.

Following the aroma of brownies to the kitchen, I found Natalie banging pots and pans and softly singing Brittany

Spears off tune.

"Wayne said to save him one of your brownies," I announced, interrupting her solo.

Natalie looked up, smiling. Ignoring my comment, she said instead, "Miss Hannah Kraeger, I am rather put-out with you. I don't think it's at all fair that you have two of the most handsome and eligible doctors on the planet in love with you. Give another girl a chance! There aren't that many decent guys out there, especially if you take two for yourself."

"I don't know what you're talking about, Natalie," I protested. "I'll lay claim to Seth, but Wayne and I are just friends. He is definitely not in love with me."

"Are you sure about that?" Natalie asked. Natalie was an incurable tease. She was never mean, but she loved to poke fun. It wasn't important whether the fun was based on facts or a complete figment of her imagination. When her professional doctor persona wasn't required, Natalie was rarely serious.

"I've seen the way he looks at you, or maybe I should say drools at you," Natalie continued. "I'm pretty sure he has a thing for his best friend's girl."

"And I think you've been watching too many soap operas," I shot back, ignoring the slightly unsettled feeling that had resurfaced with her talk. "*General Hospital* isn't real! Dr. Wayne Hawkins loves me as a close friend. He would never go after Seth's girl. Besides, he and Katherine still have their dysfunctional relationship going. Last I heard, they were on again."

Natalie rolled her eyes. "The man who keeps chasing

after Katherine will deserve what he catches. I can't stand that woman."

Natalie hadn't told me the details of her quick trip to Hawaii with Katherine, but, from what I gathered, it had not gone well. Natalie was kind of the opposite of a cheerleader for team Katherine.

"So, Mr. Five Star Chef wants one of my brownies?" Natalie said, finally returning to my initial statement. Bringing up the Katherine subject was one of the few things that could snap Natalie out of tease mode. "I'll have to call and brag to Sicily. She always claimed I couldn't follow a recipe to save my life. Shows what she knows."

"I think you are great at preparing food, Natalie," I encouraged. "Wayne's right. Those brownies do smell wonderful. And I've never heard anyone who can pick up the phone and order takeout quite the way you do."

Natalie laughed. "Speaking of takeout, the Chinese food should be delivered about 7:00. Is that okay?"

"Yes. Dad was going to drop Mom and Abby off here before going to the game with his buddies. He won't be home until really late so we should have plenty of time for Chick Flicks and chocolate. By the way, Natalie, thank you for letting my parents and Abby stay tonight,"

"No problem. Mi casa es su casa." The phrase sounded absolutely hilarious with her British accent, and I fought bursting into laughter.

I guess it wasn't technically Natalie's house, but she had lived here since she entered medical school. Natalie did not come from a wealthy family, but they did have very generous friends in high places. These friends had sponsored a lot of Natalie's education and also let her live in their San Francisco townhouse at a seriously reduced rent. They claimed she was actually helping them by taking care of it since they rarely visited, but now they were talking about the possibility of simply letting Natalie purchase it from them.

The house was much nicer than anything Natalie could have afforded as a medical student, and it would even be a stretch on her current OB/GYN salary. It was a very large, beautiful townhouse in a great location near the hospital. It even had a view of the bay from the rooftop patio. Everything from the oven range to the toilets was top-of-the-line. Sicily had lived here with Natalie for years before heading to the east coast for her fellowship. Now, I inhabited one of the beautiful rooms and enjoyed Natalie's friendship and hospitality.

"You'll be able to stick around tonight, right?" I asked.

Natalie shrugged. "I should be, but you never know. There is another doctor on call tonight. I have one patient who's due pretty soon, but I don't think it'll be tonight."

If Natalie's patient went into labor, I knew Natalie would probably be the one to deliver the baby, whether or not she was on call. Natalie was one of those rare physicians who was probably too dedicated to her patients. She really cared about them and was almost possessive. She said after investing nine months in helping a mother prepare for a moment, she didn't want someone else to take her place at the finish line. She wanted to be the one to usher in that new life. This made her schedule very unpredictable, as she could be called to deliver a baby at any time, day or night. But, she never seemed to mind. She loved her job.

The doorbell rang. "That's got to be Mom and Abby now!"

Excited, I opened the door for our smiling, enthusiastic guests. They were well-laden with luggage and a couple boxes, looking like they might stay a month instead of just a weekend.

After giving Dad a quick hug, he rushed off to his game, and I took Mom and Abby upstairs to show them where they'd be staying.

"I'm sorry Tom couldn't join us for the weekend," I told Abby. "But, at least that means you get to share a room with me. It's been a long time since we've had a slumber party!"

At the mention of Tom, Abby's smile dimmed slightly and a shadow crossed her face. Abby had never been good at masking her feelings, especially around me. I knew her too well. Sometimes I felt I knew Abby better than myself. I made a mental note to privately ask Mom what was going on with Tom.

By the time Mom and Abby had settled their things in their rooms, the Chinese food arrived. We sat around the dining room table eating sweet and sour chicken, chow mein, and egg rolls while laughing hysterically at some of Natalie's stories of her more colorful patients from medical school and her residency. I could already tell this was going to be a great evening.

"I was so nervous and confused that the Brit in me came out full force," Natalie was saying with bright eyes relishing her own story. "I told her that she needn't worry. It was just a simple procedure and Bob's your uncle. To a Brit, 'and Bob's your uncle,' is a common phrase meaning 'and that's that.' Obviously, not understanding, the poor woman asked, 'What does my Uncle Bob have to do with a pap smear?'"

Before I could let loose a peal of laughter, Mom interrupted, asking in a tight voice, "Where did you get that necklace?"

The laughter dying before it could make it through my lips, my gaze swerved to my mother's pale face and eyes focused on the tiny gold locket peeking from beneath my shirt.

I knew I shouldn't wear it. Dad had never given it to me in this timeline. But, I couldn't part with it. I now understood that it had belonged to my biological mother. It was always around my neck, but I was usually good at keeping it hidden beneath the collar of my shirt. Sometimes I would reach up and touch it, remembering the adoring looks Karis gave her baby girl—me. The locket was the only tangible connection I had to my mother and her great love for me.

Surprised by Mom's question, I reached up and fingered the locket, momentarily speechless.

"Where did you get the locket, Hannah," Mom repeated into the silent room.

Obviously surprised by Mom's abrupt question and my hesitation, Abby and Natalie were silent as they watched us. Abby knew minimal details of my latest time traveling episode. Mom and Dad had thought it best to keep her in the dark about the facts that I traveled to the future and was actually her adopted sister. Abby was typically an emotional and very transparent person. She was not good at keeping secrets. Mom and Dad thought it kinder and safer to not give her all the information. She only knew that I'd traveled again, but Seth and Wayne had developed a medication that was effective in treating me. So far, that explanation had been enough, and I had managed to avoid her trademark nosiness.

Glancing at the curiosity on both women's faces, I whispered to Mom, "Can we talk about it later?"

"No, Hannah, I need to know right now." Mom didn't sound angry, but her tone did sound upset and determined.

"Would you excuse us a moment, Natalie and Abby?" I asked. Then, realizing I was going to have to provide some information to satisfy their curiosity, I added, "Dad actually gave the necklace to me, but I think it looks very similar to one that Mom has seen before. That's why she's a little confused about it. I'll explain, and we'll be right back."

Following me to the living room, Mom asked, "Dad gave you the necklace? Why would he do that without telling me?"

"Mom," I said, trying to keep my voice quiet. "It's a little more complicated than that. Dad gave me the necklace in a different timeline. I only still have it because I was wearing it when I went back in time and this new timeline was created." I hadn't ever told mom that she was dead in the original timeline, and I really didn't want to do that now. "I know it belonged to my biological mother, Karis."

Mom sat heavily into a chair and rubbed her temples. "So, no one in this timeline ever gave you a necklace like that?"

"No."

"And, in either timeline, have you ever seen any of the other papers and things that were with you as a baby in the time machine?"

My eyes widened. "No. I mean, you showed me the letter that I wrote, but nothing else."

"I'm such an idiot," Mom groaned. Then taking a deep breath, she looked at me. "Along with that letter, the adoption papers, and instructions that were with you when we found you, there were also pictures of you as a newborn, that necklace, and a letter addressed to you. Our instructions said not to give you the letter until and unless you had full knowledge of your birth and how you came to be our daughter. Your dad and I didn't understand it at all because, as you know, we were also given specific instructions not to tell you. We didn't know how you'd ever find out if we didn't tell you. As a result, we kind of dismissed it.

"I had previously taken out the baby pictures, which I know you've seen, and the letter that I already showed you. But, I put all of your other things in a box and hid it. I should have given it to you immediately when you first returned two weeks ago, but, with all of the excitement, I honestly didn't remember that the things existed. I'm sorry, Hannah, I should have given you the necklace and the letter right away. I've always thought of you as my daughter, and, at some point, it stopped occurring to me that a different mother gave birth to you."

"Don't feel bad, Mom." I consoled. "It's only been two weeks. That was the box you brought in with your suitcase? We could go right now and look at the stuff, if that would make you feel better."

Mom nodded. "We should. I seem to recall that there

was a date on the letter from your mother as well, but I don't remember when it was."

Walking up the stairs, I was excited. A letter from Karis!

"I'm sorry if I startled you about the necklace, Hannah," Mom apologized. "I was just so surprised to see it around your neck. I hadn't seen it in probably close to twenty years, but it's so unique I recognized it right away. I couldn't imagine how you could have gotten it. I had brought the box for you today, but I hadn't stopped to really remember what was inside. Seeing the necklace triggered the memory of everything, and now I realize there might be something important."

In the guest room, Mom pulled out a small box and handed it to me. Lifting the lid, I found a bunch of slightly yellowed papers and an exact replica of the necklace I was currently wearing. I guess, in a technical sense, they were actually the same locket, just from two different timelines. I really didn't want to think that hard to analyze the cosmic implications; I'd leave the time travel theory junk to Wayne. He was going to love this.

Shuffling through the papers, I found an envelope that read "Hannah."

"I think my note with the instructions is right under it," Mom said, looking over my shoulder.

Scanning the note to Mom, I read pretty much what she had already told me. The only new information was at the bottom where it said the letter had to be given to Hannah before the date written on the envelope. It might only be a matter of days beforehand, but it was of utmost importance that date not pass without Hannah reading this letter.

Picking up my envelope again, I looked at the small print in the right hand corner. It was today's date.

"Oh no!" I heard Mom breathe behind me, and I knew she had just realized the same thing I had.

Ripping open the letter quickly, I started reading, my sense of dread growing with each word that flew past my eyes.

Dearest Hannah,

Earlier today, I watched my beautiful adult daughter disappear before my eyes. Now, I will watch that same baby girl disappear once again. I don't understand how you came or how you left. All I know is that if you hadn't, I don't think I would have had the strength or the faith to do what I must.

At least now I understand my own past better and have a glimpse into the future. When you said your name, I finally understood. There has only ever been one Hannah. But, the life you will lead is still a mystery to me. I don't know how you will save my family before I am born or how you will show up here when we need you most. I do know you will grow into a healthy, intelligent, beautiful, heroic young woman.

Blame it on my over-protective mothering instincts, but I must confess that after seeing you earlier today, I couldn't resist using a few resources to look you up. It had never occurred to me as a possibility before, but now I know you will successfully go back in time.

I don't know the ethics of time travel. I don't know if it is right to use future knowledge to change the past. However, as your mother, I can't in good conscience, let you leave my arms without warning you of what the future holds for you. I can't knowingly let you face that kind of pain when I may have done something to prevent it.

From what I have read about you, you fall in love with a man named Dr. Seth McAllister. My dear Hannah, Dr. Seth McAllister is killed in a tragic mugging on the date listed on this envelope. I have written the address and approximate time at the bottom of this page, as was listed in the newspaper account I read. From what I could find out, he was walking to his car when he was stabbed in what was called an apparent random act of violence.

I don't know what to advise you to do. I DO NOT want you intervening and getting yourself killed. I just thought that if you knew, maybe you could prevent him from being near the South San Francisco area that night. I will leave the best course of action up to my wise daughter.

According to everything I could find, you are never the same after Seth dies. You are successful, you live your life, but grief takes a tremendous toll on you. Forgive me, but I will do everything in my power to shield my daughter from such a loss.

By your appearance earlier today, I am only guessing that the fate of losing your Seth has not yet happened. I did not see the sorrow on your face that is plainly visible in pictures of you afterward.

One thing I choose to believe is that the future is not set in stone. It is changeable. Every person's actions and choices create a future that could be completely different if one person said 'no' instead of 'yes' or turned right instead of left. The future I read of you today need not be the exact future you make for yourself.

I have one added benefit of being on this end of the timeline. In a few days, after we have staged your death and funeral, I can look up my daughter and hold you in my arms one more time. Even though you will be at least twenty years older than me, you are still mine. You, on the other hand, will have to wait. Don't come to me. I will not know who you are, and you have the potential of messing things up if you are too involved in my life at any point. We will make up for lost time later.

Remember, Hannah, there is not a place or time you can go where I will not love you.

Love,

Your Mother, Karis Lawson Blake

P.S. My locket is perfect on you. I am sending it with you in hope that it will remind you of how much your mother loves you. You should probably know, however, that the locket was given to me as a gift when I was a baby. A mysterious family friend sent it to me. Her name was Hannah.

My heart was pounding. I made myself read every last excruciating word of the letter, instinctively knowing I would need every last detail Karis could provide. Finishing, I quickly looked at the information she had printed at the bottom of the paper.

My heart stopped. A scream caught in my suddenly constricted throat.

Frantic, I looked at my watch.

I didn't explain. I didn't even breathe. I ran for the door, the nightmarish letter still grasped tightly in my hand.

My weak legs wobbled as I flew down the stairs, sheer overwhelming panic chasing at my heels. I heard mom's confused voice yelling my name. But I didn't stop.

Thirty minutes. Seth would be dead in thirty minutes.

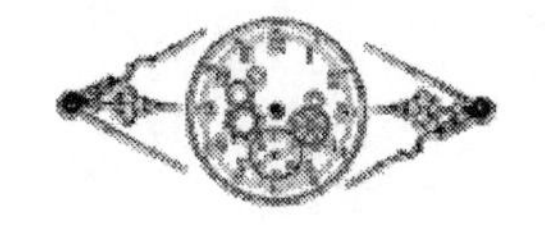

Chapter Eleven

I screamed and hit the steering wheel with my fists. Seth wasn't answering his cell phone. What was I going to do?

Breaking every speed limit sign I passed, I drove frantically through the streets of San Francisco. The address on Karis's letter wasn't really that far, but traffic and the stoplights slowed me down.

My heart was racing, my palms were sweating, and I tried to focus on not hyperventilating. The risk of time traveling again crossed my mind briefly, but I dismissed it. I couldn't think about it right now. Besides, trying to control my emotions would be pointless anyway.

Wayne's medicine would work. It had to.

Seth was going to die unless I got to him in time.

I pushed redial for about the tenth time and once again

heard Seth's cell phone go straight to voice mail. *Please, God, help me!* I begged, my breath coming in shorter gasps as sobs threatened to choke me.

I breathed out slowly. *Think, Hannah! Think!* I ordered myself. What was I going to do? I couldn't really call the police and tell them that a mugging would take place and end in someone's death in exactly fifteen minutes. I couldn't explain how I knew, and, with such a far-fetched story, they'd probably think I was loony and not take me seriously.

On the other hand, how was I going to stop someone who was armed and dangerous? Fifteen minutes. Could I even make it to the address in time? If I did, I still wouldn't have time to locate Seth and get him out of there before the mugging took place.

It was dusk. The sun was rapidly slipping behind the not-too-distant ocean, and with it, my hope seemed to be following. It seemed as if I was hitting every single red light, and traffic seemed unusually heavy.

I glanced at my watch again. Ten minutes. My thoughts bounced like a ball in a pinball machine as I tried to find some hope. People called in tips all the time. If I could just find a way to get the police to the address without revealing everything I knew… That was it! An anonymous tip! I didn't know if the police could make it there in time either, but I had to try.

Grabbing my cell phone again, my shaking fingers fumbled through dialing 911. I kind of wished a cop would see me talking on my cell phone while driving and try to pull me over. Unfortunately, a cop wouldn't be around now that I was purposely breaking multiple laws and wanting to get caught.

"911. What is your emergency?"

"I would like to call in an anonymous tip," I said simply. "I have strong reason to believe a man who's armed and dangerous is at this address. He is intending on mugging and possibly harming someone right away. Please send help quickly." I then gave the address and hung up. I didn't want to answer any questions.

I was getting close. Turning a corner, I looked around frantically, knowing the address I was searching for should be in view. I saw it and my heart stopped beating a moment before resuming at a thunderous pace. The address was a parking garage.

Now I knew, despite my tip, the police would never be able to help Seth in time. I had no idea what level Seth was parked on or where the attack would take place. Waves of helplessness washed over me. Seth was going to die, and I could do nothing to stop it.

I glanced at the clock. Five minutes. I counted four spacious levels in the parking garage. As my SUV entered the structure, I breathed a prayer that was just one word over and over: *Please!*

The last rays of the setting sun failed to illuminate the dark interior of the garage. Exceeding the five mile-per-hour speed limit, I anxiously scanned the vehicles I passed on either side as they crossed through my headlights set on bright. I didn't know what type of businesses this parking garage served, but it was still pretty full even after 8:00 at night.

Nearing the end of the second level, I saw it! A silver

BMW convertible was parked near the end of the aisle, by the turn that led up a ramp to the third level. Backing up, I parked in an open space toward the middle of the aisle.

My shaking fingers pulled the keys out of the ignition, and I had a moment's hesitation. What was I going to do? Time was up. I had no hope the police would find the right spot or even be here. I didn't know if Seth would be killed on this level. It could happen as he was entering the garage or in the elevator or… anywhere. Even if this was the right place, how could I save him? I had no weapon. The words from Karis's letter flashed through my head: "I DO NOT want you intervening and getting yourself killed."

Closing my eyes, I took a deep breath that choked out in a sob. I didn't know what I could do to save Seth, but, sitting there, I realized I did know one thing I could not do. I couldn't do nothing. If I had the slightest chance to save him, I had to try, even if it resulted in my own death. At this point, I couldn't imagine living my life without him anyway.

Jumping out of the driver's seat, I ran and opened the rear. In the dim light from an overhead light, I saw the emergency travel kit my dad had given me for my birthday. It didn't contain a weapon, but it was all I had. Fingers shaking, I opened the plastic lid, reached both hands in and grabbed the first two things they came in contact with. My right hand pulled out a large flashlight, my left hand a rope.

Closing the rear door, I turned to find the Exit sign. If the attack took place here, Seth would be coming up the stairs or the elevator to return to his car. Seeing the sign almost directly across from Seth's car, I cautiously walked around to the front of the parked cars.

Trying to eliminate any echo from my shoes on the

pavement, I started making my way toward Seth's car. There were still quite a few vehicles in this area, but it was empty of any of their owners. Overhead, dim orange lights illuminated small circles at regular intervals. The air was muggy, unusually warm for an evening in San Francisco.

The silence of the garage was ominous, the darkness oppressive. If I was right, there was a very dangerous man lurking somewhere very near. My breath came in short gasps. Here I was in a bustling city, and the only sounds I heard were the buzzing of one of the orange lights and the rapid beating of my own frightened heart.

Reaching Seth's car, I crouched down near the front driver's side, waiting and listening. What felt like hours was actually only a few seconds. I heard a sound! Footsteps echoed against the cement as they trudged up the stairs across from me. Straightening, I tried to catch a glimpse of the figure emerging from the stairwell. Was it Seth?

Suddenly, backlit against the orange glow from the stairwell, I saw the figure grabbed from behind. I heard a struggle and saw both shadows disappear as the attacker drew his victim away from the light.

My entire body felt like a bolt of lightning had seared through it. Frantic, I ran across the empty space between the rows of cars. Trying to stay low and let a minivan hide me from view, I crept to where I had seen the figures disappear. Peeking around the front of the vehicle, I thought I saw two darker shapes crowded against the wall about fifteen feet away.

"The wallet, but not the sack, huh?" a rough voice whispered with a raspy laugh. "Doesn't matter. I'll just take it off your dead body."

Not stopping to think what I was doing, I jumped from behind the minivan. Pushing the button on the big flashlight in my hand, I shined it directly at the two figures and yelled in a loud voice.

"Police! Drop your weapon and let the man go! We have you surrounded!"

Dad had been right. The flashlight was like the nuclear weapon of flashlights. It was easy to see how it could act as a flare. In its powerful beam I could see the assailant still had Seth from behind with a knife to his throat. Adjusting the beam slightly, I shined it directly in the man's eyes, knowing it was so bright, he wouldn't be able to see me or anything else, probably for a while even after the flashlight was turned off. The man groaned with the pain of the light and reached up with his free hand to rub his eyes. Still, he didn't release Seth.

I hadn't consciously thought this plan through. I didn't really know where the words were coming from. I was reacting on impulse.

At any second, the man could call my bluff and end Seth's life. I could do nothing. The knife glinted in the glare of the light as the man shifted his position slightly.

"I said drop your weapon and let the man go!" I yelled, having a hard time believing that the authoritative voice was my own. "We have three bullets aimed directly at your head. It's your choice. If you kill him, your body will beat his to the ground. If you so much as breathe wrong, you won't live to hear us say 'Oops.' I'll give you one more chance. If you want to be breathing ten seconds from now, LET HIM GO!"

"Okay, okay!" the assailant said. "Don't shoot! I'm putting the knife down."

As the man released his hold, Seth jumped away, out of the beam of the flashlight.

"Good," I said, "Now keep your hands where I can see them. Stay right where you are, nice and steady."

Keeping the light directly in his eyes, I slowly walked forward. Seeing Seth out of the corner of my eye, I held out the rope and motioned him with a tip of my head. "Would you please do the honors, McAllister?" I asked.

About the only knot I knew how to tie was the one you tie your shoelaces with. I figured Seth knew how to tie knots for sutures; he had to be more skilled than me to tie someone's hands up with a rope.

Incredulous and obviously expecting more backup than just me, Seth still silently obeyed my orders. Keeping the beam directly on the man's closed eyes, I kicked the knife further away, while Seth put the man's hands behind his back and swiftly tied knots a sailor would be proud of.

"What the…?" The assailant questioned. "Rope? No handcuffs? What is this?"

Before I could think of a plausible answer, sirens split the air. Red and blue lights danced up the ramp to the second level as three police cars came into view. Seeing my flashlight beam that I'm sure could also be viewed from space, they screeched to a stop.

Officers suddenly surrounded us, asking questions. Numb with a mixture of shock and relief, I couldn't seem to find words to answer their questions. Quickly assessing the situation, even without my explanation, they took Seth's attacker into custody. It felt as if I was watching everything from behind a glass. My muscles turned to mush, and I sank to the cold pavement.

After talking with the officers a few minutes, Seth came and knelt beside me. He gently pried my fingers off the flashlight still in my hand and turned it off.

"Hannah, sweetheart," he said, gently caressing my face. "Are you okay?"

Blinking as his image registered in my numb brain, I said the first thing that came to mind. "Where is your cell phone?" I asked.

A knife had been to Seth's throat only minutes before. He'd almost been killed. Yet the first question I asked was 'Where is your cell phone.' In my defense, even I had the presence of mind to realize I was in shock.

Seth's smile of relief turned a bit sheepish. "I forgot it at work."

Blinking again, my mind came further back into the present. "Seth, are you okay?" I asked anxiously. "Did he hurt you?"

I reached out and lightly ran my fingers over his face and his neck, looking for injuries and finding none in the dim light. Suddenly, I was enfolded in the pair of strong arms I had feared I'd never again feel around me.

"I was so scared," I moaned. "I thought I was going to lose you."

"Ssshhh," Seth whispered. "I'm fine. Thanks to you, my

brave Hannah, I'm fine."

An officer came over to talk to us, and we got to our feet. He suggested we come down to the station where we could give a full statement.

Driving first to Seth's work a few blocks away, we left my SUV there, and I drove with Seth the rest of the way. By the time we got to the station, I had filled him in on most of the details as to how I'd come to the parking garage.

Enclosed in a small, windowless room with an older officer whose manner seemed more machinelike than human, I tried to stick as close to the truth as possible. I said I had been driving through the parking garage when I had seen Seth's car. I didn't know why he was there, but I'd decided to try to find him. I had gotten out of the car and seen the attacker grab Seth. Grabbing the first things I could find out of the back of my vehicle, I'd run and acted on the first solution that popped into my head—a massive bluff.

Seth had already given his statement, and was now holding my hand, trying to shift some of the focus off questions in my direction.

"How did you guys happen to show up?" Seth asked the questioning officer, after I'd given my brief outline of events. I hadn't had a chance to fill him in on all of the details of my rescue mission.

"We received an anonymous tip about an armed man intent on committing a crime at that location. We were hesitant to respond, but the dispatcher had thought the woman calling had sounded legitimate. We hadn't had time to get a full trace on the call, but we did know it came from the same general area as the address given."

Another officer entered the small room where we were seated. I recognized him as the one Seth had talked to at the scene. He was an overweight fellow who was as animated as the other officer was lethargic. Overhearing what his coworker had said, he jumped in to finish the tale.

"It's kind of a slow night. We had some officers available, so we decided to go in with sirens blaring. We didn't know where exactly the perp might be, but we figured, at the very least, we could scare him up a bit. Now, of course we're glad we decided to follow up on the tip. We figure it either came from someone who knew the perp or a witness who saw him entering the parking garage."

"So, do you have any more information on the attacker?" Seth asked. I could tell he was trying to keep the conversation from returning to the details of my side of the story.

"No surprise there," he announced. "He has a rap sheet about a mile long. He's a pro at this. He lawyered-up quick and is not saying a word. He'll probably take a plea, and it'll never go to trial. I don't think either of you will be given the chance to testify."

"So you didn't learn anything about why he attacked me?" Seth asked.

"Not really. As I said, he's keeping his mouth shut. All the evidence suggests that it was random. The other crimes in his history were random as well. He probably saw what you bought and followed you. I know you were concerned that you may have been targeted for some reason, but I really don't think that's the case. He's just a really bad guy who doesn't care if he kills someone or not. He probably has committed numerous other robberies and crimes that we can't pin on him."

Seth nodded thoughtfully.

The officer then turned his jolly eyes on me, speaking with frank admiration. "You need to be thankful that this brave little lady happened by at the right time. I still can't believe you managed to bluff a dangerous criminal into standing down using only a flashlight and some rope. I've never heard anything like it."

I felt a blush starting to heat up my cheeks.

"You know this is the kind of story that the media would love," he mused with a mischievous glint in his eye.

"Oh, please don't release it to the press," I begged, panicking at the thought of having to answer reporters' pointed questions. "I really don't want the attention, and I wouldn't want someone else to try to pull a similar stunt and get killed."

"I can't make any promises that they won't somehow find out," he answered, slightly deflated, "but, if they do, it certainly won't be from me." Thankfully, the officer seemed honest and understanding of my concerns.

Both officers then thanked us for our time and said we were free to go. They would be in contact if they needed anything else.

As the friendly officer escorted us to the lobby, my cell phone rang. I answered my mom's frantic call while Seth talked to the officer a few more minutes.

"Hannah, where are you?" Mom asked. "I've been trying to call you. What's going on?"

Guiltily, I realized that I'd been so distracted, I had ignored her calls and sent several straight to voicemail. She hadn't read the letter from Karis, giving me privacy of reading it alone the first time. She had no idea what the letter said or why I'd run off in such an obvious panic.

As quickly and briefly as possible, I explained I'd learned that Seth was in trouble, and I had to go help him. I assured her that we were both fine, and I'd fill her in on the details when I got back to Natalie's house.

Unfortunately, my brief explanation wasn't good enough for Mom.

"Where are you now, Hannah? When will you be home?"

Biting my lip in frustration, I realized that I couldn't avoid answering her unless I wanted to outright lie, which I couldn't do. Honesty, especially with my parents, was too ingrained in me. Sighing, I answered, "We're at the police station here in San Francisco."

"The police station!" Mom shrieked. "Hannah, you HAVE to tell me what's going on."

"The excitement is all over, Mom. We're wrapping things up. I really can't talk about it now, but I promise I'll answer all of your questions when I get there."

"When will that be?" She asked impatiently.

I sighed again. I knew Seth was going to want to talk before we had to explain everything to my family. Other than the brief explanation on the way here, we hadn't had time to discuss what had happened.

"Give me an hour and a half," I said, knowing that Mom

would be satisfied with nothing less than an exact answer. "Seth and I need to tie up a few loose ends. I don't know if he's even had dinner. I know it'll be late, but that's the best I can do. If you want to go to bed, I can fill you in tomorrow."

"No, Hannah, I'll be up. Take your time."

I felt a wave of love for my sweet mom. I knew how difficult it was for her to wait.

"Oh, and Mom," I said, remembering something. "What about Abby and Natalie? What did you tell them?"

"I told them you were called away on an emergency. They know nothing about the letter. They went ahead with the movies, but they know I've been a nervous wreck. They're very curious, so you'll have to think of something to tell them. I figured the less they knew, the better. Abby just about can't take it, though. I keep avoiding being alone with her. Natalie's presence is the only thing making her mind her manners and not resume the Inquisition."

I smiled. My mom was the best. "Thank you, Mom. I'll see you in a little bit. Love you. Bye."

I would have to think of some really good excuse for Abby. I wasn't really worried about Natalie, but Abby wouldn't be put off easily. Luckily, Mom could help run interference.

Winding my fingers through Seth's, we exited the building. Waves of relief coursed through me. Seth must have felt my legs wobble going down the steps. He placed his arm around me, pulling me close as we walked to his car.

I had done it! I had saved Seth! The bad guy was in custody, Seth was safe, and, I suddenly realized, my medication had worked! I had never been so scared in my life, yet I had not time traveled. As intense relief coursed through my body, my legs couldn't seem to work. Seth swung me up in his arms and carried me the last few steps to the car. I was free.

CHAPTER TWELVE

IT was a beautiful night. The fog hadn't rolled in from the ocean yet, and the lights outlining the spans of the Golden Gate Bridge were beautiful against a background of velvet black. Sitting on a bench overlooking the bay, Seth and I were silent, letting the peaceful beauty ease some of the residual tension before having to relive what had happened.

After leaving the station, Seth hadn't wanted to eat, saying he still had too much adrenaline running through him to be hungry. Instead, he had driven to this secluded spot to decompress and talk. It was the perfect place. Looking at the beautiful view, time seemed momentarily paused, and it was hard to believe that the evil we had just experienced even existed.

Snuggling closer to Seth in the cool air, he wrapped an arm around me. Almost directly overhead, a full moon hung suspended like a lighted Christmas ornament. Looking up, the moon silhouetted the outline of the face I loved. Reaching with my fingers, I gently stroked his face and neck. He flinched in pain.

"Seth, you're hurt!" I said straightening.

"I'm fine, Hannah."

Without a word, I marched the few steps back to the car and retrieved a small flashlight from the glove compartment. Returning to Seth, he reluctantly consented as I conducted a flashlight examination of his injuries. I was mad at myself for not noticing anything earlier. The light had been too dim in the parking garage, and I guess I'd been too distracted in the police station to notice the redness around his neck. There was also a slight line, not a cut, but a pressure mark like something had been pressed hard against his neck.

When I finally clicked off the flashlight, he pulled me close and said, "See, it's nothing. I'm fine. I might be stiff and a little bruised tomorrow, but that's it. I'm alive… thanks to you."

Burying his face in my hair, he whispered, "You were magnificent Hannah! I can't believe you did that!" He groaned. "I feel so conflicted! I want to tell you how foolish you were to have put yourself in harm's way like that. You had nothing to defend yourself. You could have very easily been killed. There's no way I would have ever wanted you to try to save me yourself. But, on the other hand, you were so smart! So brave! If you hadn't been there…"

"You would have died." I finished, shivering. "There's no question of that. According to my mom's letter, you did die. I don't know the ethics of time travel, but this is one event I do not regret changing. I had to do something, Seth. It was too late to stop it, and I couldn't sit around and let you die. I couldn't have handled it if you had… " Tears choked my voice and I couldn't continue.

"Shh," Seth comforted. "I'm fine. You're stuck with me now. I'm not going to leave."

Thinking of how scared I'd been and how very close I'd come to losing this man, I cried. All my pent-up emotion was released in tears as Seth cradled me against his chest. The steady beat of his heart calmed me. It was a beat that should have stopped about 90 minutes ago. Now, it sounded so steady, the arms around me felt so strong. He was alive.

It still scared me that I didn't know what tomorrow might bring. Because of Karis's letter, I had saved him, but that didn't guarantee I wouldn't lose him tomorrow some other way.

My mind relived the moments in the parking garage when I thought he was going to be killed. Suddenly rising out of Seth's arms, I pushed him away hard.

"Ow!" Seth exclaimed. "What was that for?"

"Why didn't you give him the sack?" I accused, remembering the attacker's words I had overheard. "Was it really worth your life? If you wouldn't have been so stubborn and stupid, you would have given him what he wanted, and I wouldn't have had to come rescue you!"

"Wait a minute!" Seth protested. "You obviously didn't hear everything."

"I heard enough!" I retorted angrily, not waiting for Seth's explanation. "I heard the bad guy say that you gave him your wallet but not the sack. He then said it didn't matter, he'd just 'take it off your dead body.'

The words as well as the man's raspy voice were ingrained in my head and would undoubtedly haunt my dreams. I shivered involuntarily. Seth reached for me, but I shied away.

"You were being mugged, Seth! You should have given him everything, including the used tissue in your pocket if he asked! Nothing is worth your life!"

I knew I was probably overreacting, but I couldn't stop myself. I would normally never use the words stupid and Seth in the same sentence, but the fear I'd felt, coupled with the realization that Seth could have prevented things from escalating, was more than I could handle.

I hoped that my medication was still effective, because I couldn't seem to control the sharp, intense anger I was feeling.

"Hannah, sweetheart," Seth said calmly. "I know you're upset, but let me explain. You heard the end of what the man said, but you apparently missed the beginning. After grabbing me, putting a knife to my throat, and pulling me out of the light, he told me to give him my wallet and the sack I had hidden in the inner pocket of my jacket. Then he laughed and said he guessed it didn't really matter if I gave them to him. I was going to die either way. If I didn't hand them over now, he'd just take them later."

The anger left me like air deflating a balloon. As I tried to wrap my mind around this new information, Seth continued. "I gave him my wallet to stall him, but not the sack. I figured giving him one, but not the other, might buy me a little time to figure out what to do. Besides, given the choice, I didn't really want to hand over the other item. I'd rather him have to take it over my dead body."

Smiling slightly, Seth looked at me. The moonlight revealed no anger over my tirade reflecting in his eyes, just compassion. I felt both ashamed of my behavior and confused by Seth's story.

Groaning in shame, I scooted close to him again and buried my face in the collar of his shirt.

"But I don't understand," I said, lifting my head. "It was a mugging. Why would he want to kill you if he got what he wanted."

Seth shrugged, not seeming to want to connect the dots for me.

Undeterred, I talked my way through my thought process. "That's why the officer at the police station mentioned you were concerned about it not being a random crime. Your attacker obviously had been watching you. He knew you had put a sack in your inside jacket pocket. If he was interested in mugging you, he should have just taken your things and left. But, he said it didn't matter, he was going to kill you anyway."

After thinking in silence a few more seconds, I finally concluded with a wave of goosebumps, "It's almost as if you were his specific target. He seemed more interested in killing you than mugging you."

Seth looked uneasy, as if he had come to the same conclusion himself, but hadn't wanted to worry me with such thoughts.

"I thought it was suspicious too," he finally admitted. "I told everything to the police. Remember what Officer Nash said? After questioning my attacker and reviewing his record, the officer was sure I was just a random target."

"But why would the guy want to kill you?"

"I talked to Officer Nash a little more about it while you were on the phone with your mom. He said that he questioned the guy pretty closely, but he wasn't talking at all until he got his lawyer. This crime seemed pretty consistent with some of the previous crimes. He said that if I had truly been a target to kill, my attacker would have to be getting paid a good amount to keep quiet and take the rap. In Nash's opinion, this criminal wasn't the type. He said he's a career criminal and doesn't really need an excuse to commit a crime, including murder."

Feeling slightly mollified, I nodded. "I guess we're going to have to be satisfied with not knowing all of the details as to why. I know Karis's letter from the future also said it was a random crime. I guess you were in the wrong place at the wrong time to meet one really bad guy."

"Don't worry about it, Hannah, I'm sure it was random. It's not like anyone has any reason to want me dead. Everybody loves me, remember?"

I smiled. I was only too aware that everyone, especially woman, loved the exceptional Dr. Seth McAllister. A thought hit me suddenly. "You're not working on anything at work that could get you in trouble, are you?"

I wasn't sure why I asked. As a general rule, Wayne and Seth didn't work on anything controversial, and I hadn't heard of any crazy disgruntled patients either past or present.

At my question, I thought I saw a strange light dawn in Seth's eyes, but he either masked it quickly or dismissed it after mentally reviewing the work aspect of his life. "No. Everything I'm working on is pretty boring. I don't really have a chance to offend somebody. At this point, I'm not working with many patients. I'm mostly just researching and testing medications."

"That's a relief," I said. "So if you're not secretly a CIA agent, there's no rogue government agency after you, and you haven't recently created or treated Frankenstein, then I think we're probably safe to suspend all conspiracy theories for now."

"Well, not the CIA, but there was this one time with the NSA…"

I laughed, feeling more like myself. We had survived and analyzed every angle. Now we could put it behind us and get back to being just Seth and Hannah.

"By the way," I said, "what were you doing in the parking garage? When Wayne came over to drop off my medication, he said you were in a meeting and then had some errands to do.

"I wouldn't have expected you to be in that parking garage. I don't even know what kind of businesses it serves."

"Just some restaurants and a few stores." Seth answered. "I was just doing a little shopping."

"For what? Your attacker had to have seen you buy something. What was in the sack anyway?"

"Sheesh, Hannah! Why do you have to know every last

detail? You have like a sixth sense for these types of things and won't be satisfied until you know all!"

I might have been offended and hurt by Seth's words, except that I saw his eyes sparkling with humor in the moonlight.

I looked up at him, feigning an overly innocent look.

Reaching out, Seth lightly tangled his fingertips in my hair and leaned forward, whispering in my ear. "And have I mentioned that I love every last curious hair on your head?"

Shivers raced down my spine at the touch of his breath on my skin. But, I knew what his goal was—distraction.

Tilting my head, I whispered seductively back in his ear. "The sack, Seth. What's in the sack?"

Straightening, Seth's groan ended in a laugh, his diversion tactic obviously unsuccessful. "Okay, Hannah, you win."

Reaching into his jacket, he pulled out a small, light-colored, sack. It was too dark for me to read the logo on it. I don't know what I expected it to hold. I had just wanted to find out what was so important for Seth to buy and then not be willing to part with. Maybe it was another charm for my bracelet. With Seth's love of surprises, I tried to make my policy preemptive in nature. A ruined surprise was a success in my book.

From inside the sack, he removed a small object and placed it in my hand. My curious fingers inspected the small, dark box. Finding a hinge, I carefully pried the lid up.

A large, beautiful diamond sparkled moonlight back at

me. It was a ring.

With a sharp intake of breath, my shocked gaze turned to find Seth, but he was no longer on the bench beside me. He was directly in front of me, kneeling on one knee. He took my left hand in his and kissed my ring finger. Looking up, his eyes shone as brilliantly as the diamond in my hand.

"Hannah Grace Blake Kraeger, I don't care what your real name is. I don't care if you were born in the future or two hundred years ago. I don't understand everything that has happened to you, and I don't know what tomorrow will bring. All I know is that I am madly, deeply, and hopelessly in love with you.

"I've loved you since the first night we met. I think you are the bravest, smartest, most beautiful, most incredible woman I've ever met. The times I thought I might lose you have been the most difficult of my life.

"My life without you makes no sense. No matter what tomorrow brings, I want to be beside you. If we have one day or sixty years, I want you to be mine. I know it won't be perfect. As we both know, time is very changeable—there are no guarantees. But, I can promise you that no one will ever love you more than I do. Please give me the opportunity to prove that love every day for the rest of our lives. Hannah, will you please marry me? Be my Hannah forever. Be my wife."

Tears rolled down my face. We hadn't really talked about marriage before. I knew how I felt about him, but I hadn't wanted to pressure him or jinx the relationship by bringing something up that he wasn't ready for. Now, I sat transfixed, not believing the words this extraordinary man was saying to me. He really wanted to marry me?

Reaching up, Seth gently caught my tears on his fingertip. “Hannah?” he asked softly.

“Yes.” I said, finally finding my voice. “Yes, Seth. I want to be your wife more than anything in the world.”

With an exuberant shout, Seth jumped up, lifted me off the bench and twirled me around. Finally setting my feet on the ground, he trailed kisses over my face, kissing away any remaining tears and ending with a long, lingering kiss on my lips.

Fortunately, I’d still managed to keep hold of the small box. Carefully, Seth removed the ring and gently slid it on my finger.

It was a huge princess cut diamond and was honestly the most beautiful ring I had ever seen. Looking at it sparkle like stars as it caught the moonlight, tears once again filled my eyes.

“This is what you bought?” I asked, remembering how he’d been willing to hang onto it until his death. “This is what the mugger wanted?”

“Yes. I had purchased the ring a while ago, but I picked it up today.”

“I had no idea that you were thinking about marrying me. You’d never mentioned…”

“Why would I need to discuss it? I knew that I wanted to marry you five-and-a-half years ago when we first met. After finding you again, there’s no way I was going to let you go.

Of course, I had to wait a respectable amount of time before proposing. I didn't want to scare you off."

"And, knowing your fondness for surprises," I added, "you couldn't resist surprising me with a ring out of the blue."

"That may have had something to do with it," Seth admitted with a smile, "but give me a little credit. This wasn't exactly how I'd planned to propose. After what happened tonight and my interrogation by Little Miss Curiosity, I had to revise things and evaluate what was important."

"I'm sorry," I said, biting my lip and feeling a little guilty over pressuring him on the sack issue. "I had no idea."

"Don't be sorry at all, my Love," he said, teasingly planting a kiss on the tip of my nose. "I got exactly what I wanted—you. What could have been the worst day of my life, turned out as the best."

Suddenly remembering my mom, and the promise I'd made to be home, I turned my watch to catch the light from the moon. "Yikes! I need to get back home. I promised to fill Mom in on the details of your attack, but now I get to tell my whole family some much better news! They're going to be so surprised!"

"Well, your dad won't be," Seth corrected. At my puzzled look, he explained. "He already knows I intend to marry you. I had to ask his permission, of course. I actually took care of that quite a while ago. He's probably starting to wonder what's taking me so long."

My heart melted at Seth's thoughtfulness. He'd asked

my dad to marry me! Wrapping my arms around him, I had no words to convey what I was feeling. I loved him so much, yet those words seemed inadequate.

With the lights from the moon and the Golden Gate as our audience, a stunning engagement ring on my finger, and Seth's arms holding me close, I had one of those perfect moments you wish you could freeze. If only time would stop for a while, I could stay and enjoy this exact minute when life and happiness seemed complete. The man of my dreams was going to marry me.

Eventually, we made it back to Natalie's house. It turned out Natalie and Abby weren't nearly as curious about my disappearance as Mom had been afraid of. They never asked a single question about it, and I didn't have to invent excuses or tell half-truths. It was almost like magic. I walked into the room, waved my left hand in front of their faces, and they forgot everything. Turns out that sparkly stone on my hand had an added benefit. It was one big and highly effective distraction.

CHAPTER THIRTEEN

REVENGE was sweet. It was the night of the grand opening gala of Wayne and Seth's research foundation, and Seth had no idea what I had in store for him. As I had promised, the man who loved surprises was about to get a taste of his own medicine.

I felt a thrill of anticipation as I entered the grand ballroom of the hotel. The beautiful and extravagant décor might not be impressive to tonight's wealthy guests and sponsors, but I felt a little like a country girl in the big city for the first time.

Large chandeliers graced the center of the room, their lights reflecting off the marble floor. Even the ceiling was an artistic masterpiece, a mural woven with gold in the romantic style. Chairs were stationed in rows in front of a stage at one end of the room. At the other end, light reflected off the glasses hanging in a small bar. A large buffet table surrounded by several white shrouded tables took up most of the space at that end. In the center of the room, a large area still remained, reserved for music and dancing later in the evening.

Seth and I had been engaged a month, and I was still getting accustomed to the idea of combining our lives. We hadn't officially set a wedding date, but we were thinking about next summer. Seth didn't really like the idea of waiting almost a year, but it would allow me to finish the graduate program I was starting soon, plan a wedding, and get used to the significant changes in my life. Seth's background was much more privileged than mine, and, in these types of settings, I still couldn't help feeling like Eliza Doolittle in *My Fair Lady.*

I scanned the large room for Seth. I had arrived early and the room was still mostly empty. A few guests in beautiful formal attire were beginning to trickle in. Seth had spent all day making last minute preparations and had asked if I would mind meeting him at the hotel instead of him picking me up.

I had been helping with preparations for the past month, but, after noon today, Seth wouldn't let me do a thing. He tried to tell me that he wanted me to have plenty of time to get ready, but I also knew that he didn't want me to know everything about tonight's event. He was always trying to have some kind of surprise up his sleeve, but tonight the surprise would be on him.

Seeing Seth talking to the caterer, I walked across the room. Turning, Seth saw me, his eyes lighting up and a wide smile dimpling his face. It still amazed me that I could have that effect on him.

"First things first," Seth said, taking my hands and leading me to a more secluded corner. Drawing me close, he breathed in my ear, "Hannah you look absolutely breathtaking."

His breath gave me goosebumps, and my heart went wild as he feathered light kisses down the side of my neck.

"Seth, knock it off!" I protested. "Someone is going to see you!"

"Let them," he responded. "They'll just be jealous that I get to kiss the most beautiful woman in the room."

I rolled my eyes. "That's not exactly a highly competitive title right now. Nobody's here yet."

"You'll still be the most beautiful woman. I didn't know you owned a dress like that. I need to take you to fancy places more often."

I was glad Seth liked the way I looked. I wore a simple black evening gown that probably wouldn't compare to the designer dresses worn by other ladies, but I felt good in it. It had an interesting neckline, an open back, and was form fitting in all the right places. Abby had lent her fashion talents to doing my makeup and sweeping my hair up into a graceful cascade of auburn curls. All in all, I was Hannah at her absolute best.

"Is everything ready?" I asked, purposely changing the subject. As much as I loved being the object of Seth's devotion, I really didn't want him to resume his appreciation. After all, we were in a public place, and I had a strong aversion to telling Seth to stop kissing me.

"We're as ready as we'll ever be. Wayne's running around here somewhere, making sure all the tech stuff is set up for his presentation. This place should be filling up soon with guests who hopefully have very deep pockets. Our sponsor has put in considerable investment, but hopefully we'll get significantly more support tonight."

"I'm sure you will," I said supportively. "You and Wayne have done an amazing job. The new research facility is beautiful. When you show everyone the slides with the pictures, the research you've already done, and your vision for the future, they'll probably want to hand you blank checks."

"I don't know about that, but having a well-known band perform and a well-stocked auction will help too."

"Gotta love those friends in high places."

"What about you?" Seth asked. "I feel like I haven't had a chance to talk to you in days. Did you get your package sent?"

I nodded. "I kept the note to Matt and Kelly brief, simply stating that the locket was for Baby Karis. I mentioned that since I'd gotten a small gift for Tim and Maddie when we visited last Christmas, I had wanted to send something for Karis as well."

After rereading Karis's letter over many times, I had known what I had to do. I had in my possession two tiny gold lockets—one from an alternate timeline that I had carried with me to this new one, and the one that my mother, Karis, had sent in the time machine with me as a baby. In essence, they were the same locket with the same history, now present in a single timeline.

I took one of the lockets, wrapped it carefully in a box, and sent it back to my mother, Matt and Kelly's baby daughter. Sending the package had left me a little depressed. I knew that it was the last contact I would have with the Lawsons. It was strange and more than a little fascinating for me to think that Matt and Kelly were my grandparents, Maddie and Tim were my aunt and uncle, and Baby Karis was my mother. My unquenchable curiosity made me wish I could know them.

"I know that I can't be a part of their lives," I explained to Seth. "It wouldn't be wise to see or contact them anymore. But, I know you and Matt are close. How are we going to cut off communication and not hurt them too badly?"

"Don't worry about it too much, Hannah. I think circumstances are going to work a natural break for us. Last time I talked to Matt, he said the family was going to be moving out of state while he did some graduate work. He anticipates coming back to the area eventually, but doesn't know when that'll be. It's going to seem natural to lose contact with us. When we get married, we'll be changing addresses and phone numbers anyway. It'll work out."

Somehow, Seth's words were less than comforting. It was difficult knowing that I had family out there that couldn't know I existed.

As if reading my thoughts, Seth said, "I know it's difficult, Hannah, but you can't risk the consequences of being part of their lives. You said yourself that the adult Karis obviously didn't recognize you. If you get involved, you risk screwing up both your life and time in general. Maybe you'll never be born."

Seth must have read the bleak look on my face, saying, "Don't feel bad, Hannah. It's not as if you won't ever see that side of your family again. It'll just be a while."

"Yeah, about thirty-five years."

"Hey, McAllister!" Wayne came by, thumping Seth on the back. "Stop talking to the lovely Hannah and start schmoozing! We need your legendary charm working overtime tonight. This place is filling up fast. I figured we'd start the presentation in about fifteen minutes."

"Duty calls!" Seth said as he obediently turned and began making his way through the guests, shaking hands and flashing brilliant smiles as he went.

"I think I saw Abby and your parents over by the food," Wayne told me. "I also saw Seth's parents arrive and head over to the stage."

"Thanks, Wayne," I said. "Are we all set up for the presentation?"

"Absolutely!" he assured with a grin and a wink. "You're going to owe me big, little lady. I would be willing to accept a dance with you later as partial payment, though."

"Your wish is my command," I said obediently.

As I walked away to find my family, I heard Wayne sigh dramatically and say, "So she says!"

It took me a while to locate my family by the food table. I wasn't used to seeing them dressed so elegantly. Mom and Abby looked gorgeous in their new evening gowns bought for the occasion. Mom's gray dress might look drab on any other woman, but it was gorgeous on her. Abby looked like a model in her off the shoulder, deep purple creation. I couldn't remember the last time I'd seen Dad in a suit. I was glad to see Tom at Abby's elbow. I hadn't seen him in a while and was glad he'd been able to make it.

Selecting a few appetizers myself, we were soon laughing and talking excitedly about the food, the glamour, and what else the evening had in store. Tom, thoroughly bored with our conversation, wandered off in the direction of the stage, probably wanting to check out the technology.

Dad's cell phone rang. Looking at the number, he answered it and immediately began weaving his way across the room to find some privacy. It wasn't unusual for Dad to receive a call on his cell phone at an inopportune time. He was a general contractor and often in demand. It was unusual for him to take a call in such a setting. He usually kept business during the workday and tried to religiously protect family time and special events.

Dad returned after several minutes, and I wasted no time voicing my curiosity. He'd had my entire life to get used to my nosiness, and I felt no shyness whatsoever.

"Who called, Dad?"

Dad didn't answer right away, but I saw a swift but meaningful glance exchanged between my parents.

"Ok, spill the beans," I said, not knowing if he intended on answering my initial question. "I'm not stupid. It must have been an important call. You don't usually take calls in these settings. What's going on?"

Sharing another long look with Mom, Dad finally sighed, but directed his answer to her. "They upped the offer on the house."

Mom nodded.

"What offer?" Abby and I asked simultaneously. Abby was just as curious as I. It's an absolute wonder that my parents were able to keep anything from two such daughters. I was still amazed that we were able to keep Abby in the dark about the full extent of my time traveling.

Apparently receiving nonverbal permission from Mom, Dad finally answered. "A few months ago, we were approached by a group wanting to purchase our house. Specifically, they want the land. They already have purchased some land that adjoins ours and made us a very good offer. We initially refused, seeing no reason to sell, but they called back and raised the offer significantly. We'd already been talking about reconsidering."

"But, what would you do?" I asked. "Where would you move?"

"There is a lot of building going on in the Sonora/Silver Springs area. I've had quite a bit of interest given the few feelers I've put out. We've talked about moving into one of the larger cabins at Silver Springs. That way, I could continue my contract business while your Mom helped Abby run the business there. I would be available to take care of any of the heavy labor on my days off."

"I could do work as a CPA on the side if we needed it," Mom added, "but, trust me, I would dearly love to make it through a tax season without high doses of caffeine."

I should have been shocked, but I wasn't. My parents loved Jackson and had never talked about moving before. However, I had already figured out that my parent's property would have to be sold sometime in the next thirty-five years.

I glanced over at Abby. She looked uncomfortable and her eyes glistened suspiciously. I wondered that Mom and Dad felt the need to "help Abby." I knew that Tom had not really been happy, especially lately, about managing Silver Springs, but I didn't really have a good handle on the situation.

"I don't want you to feel like you have to do this," Abby said in a small voice, seeming to have trouble conveying her thoughts. "If it's something you *want* to do, I will be… relieved. You know that Tom wants to do more computer consulting, maybe even some traveling. If you were there to carry some of the load… it would help."

I was surprised. Abby was notoriously independent. If she was willing to accept such large-scale assistance from Mom and Dad, things might be worse than I thought.

"You said a 'group' wanted to buy your property?" Abby asked, directing the conversation to more emotionally stable ground. "What will they do with it?"

"They want to build a medical research facility," Dad answered. "I'm not sure why they targeted our town as a good location, but I know it would be a very good move for the economy of Jackson."

I hadn't told my parents all of the details of my trip to the future. I also don't think they fully comprehended the details of my time traveling to realize that I always traveled to the same physical location as I left, just a different time. The fact that a research company wanted to build a facility on their property was a complete surprise to them.

"What is this company's name?" Abby asked. "Have I

heard of them before?"

"Intrepid," I answered without thinking. Three pairs of eyes swerved to me in surprise.

"How did you know?" Mom asked.

"I guess I ran across it somewhere," I said, trying to pass it off with a nonchalant shrug.

"That's funny," Dad answered. "I was told that they were keeping everything quiet until they could make a formal announcement as to plans and a completion date."

Everyone, Mom especially, was still looking at me with suspicion.

"Oh, look," I said, with more than a little relief. "I think I see Wayne signaling me. It's probably time for me to make the introduction for the presentation."

It was show time, I thought excitedly. Sure, it was time for the big presentation about the Hawkins and McAllister Research Company, but it was also time for my promised revenge.

A while back, Seth had let it slip that he hated public speaking. I had found this amazing and rather humorous. Seth was so charming and good with people that anyone would assume he would shine as a public speaker, but apparently not. Seth had insisted that Wayne do all of the presenting and speaking tonight while he ran things behind the scenes.

I had called him a wimp, especially since I had agreed to give the introduction. Public speaking was definitely not my forte, but I was willing to pitch in for the greater good. Seth was not.

Needing an accomplice, I had recruited Wayne. He had been more than willing, assuring me that Seth was fully capable of giving the presentation. He said that Seth was actually a good speaker, but he had an intense dislike for it. With my nagging doubts assuaged by Wayne, we had set the plan in motion.

Now, standing on stage myself, I realized I wasn't going to get out of this without an attack of overactive nerves. My palms began to sweat, my heart got a head start at the racetrack, and I felt the muscles holding my smile begin to twitch.

Come on, Hannah! I told myself. *If you can manage to deliver a baby, travel through time, and save people's lives on multiple occasions, you can handle a little speech!*

Throughout everything, I had learned that I was much more capable than I had ever believed. Unfortunately, I hadn't also acquired an enjoyment of public speaking or a cure for my disloyal nerves along the way.

I can do this! With determination, I took the microphone, put on my most charming persona, and invited all of the guests to be seated for the upcoming presentation.

"We would like to thank all of you for attending tonight." I said. "This event represents both the culmination of a lot of work and the birth of a dream. Dr. Wayne Hawkins and Dr. Seth McAllister have worked tirelessly to create a foundation like no other. Tonight, we would like to present you with a sample of the work we have done so far, share our unique philosophy of research, and hope that you will share this dream for the future with us. To this end, it is my pleasure to introduce one of our country's most talent and gifted physicians, co-founder of Hawkins and McAllister Research, Dr. Seth McAllister."

The plan, as far as Seth knew, was for me to announce Wayne. Looking to the back of the seating area where Seth was positioned to help with the technology, I wanted to giggle at the look of surprise on my fiancé's face. Recovering quickly, Seth stood and strode up to the stage.

Feeling especially naughty, I added one more thing before passing the microphone over. "Oh, and a little bird told me that the multi-talented Dr. McAllister might also have prepared a vocal performance to share with us later."

Not wanting to look at Seth's face for fear of bursting into laughter, I thrust the microphone at him, exited the stage, and made my way to a seat in back. After clearing his throat and greeting everyone, I looked up in time to see Seth remove a paper from his back pocket and flash his most charming smile… at me.

"You'll have to excuse me," he said. "I'm a doctor, not a public speaker." After the laughter following his fairly decent impersonation of Dr. McCoy from Star Trek, he continued. "I would be completely lost had I not had a chance to write some notes for myself."

Seth then launched into a beautifully crafted, expertly delivered speech. He was funny in all the right places, making boring Power Point slides and research reports interesting and easy to follow.

After listening in shock for several minutes, I had to face the truth. Seth had obviously prepared. I had been duped. Seth had known that he, not Wayne, was going to be giving the presentation.

Turning around in my seat, I immediately met Wayne's eyes as he was standing in that back in Seth's former position. His dark eyes shining with great amusement, he slowly and deliberately raised his hand and saluted me.

Turning back around, I crossed my arms in front of me and closed my eyes, trying to block out the beautiful, charming tenor of my infuriating fiancé's voice. I had been so sure I had given him a most deserving surprise! Now, I realized that the surprise was for me… again!

Feeling a touch on my shoulder, I turned to find Wayne at my elbow. Handing me something, he bent and whispered in my ear.

"Seth asked that I give you these. He said you might need it. He mentioned something about how you like to doodle when you're upset. Maybe you could use it to take some notes."

With a wink, he pushed two small objects in my hand and returned to his post. I looked down to find a pen and a clipboard. Held on the clipboard was a large, white napkin.

I should have been furious. It was almost like they were rubbing my nose in the fact that they had outmaneuvered me. Instead, I found myself suppressing giggles. I couldn't be mad at them. My sense of humor was always my downfall.

Turning the napkin over, I found a small doodle already there. It was a heart with the words 'Seth loves Hannah' inside. My heart melting, I contentedly settled down to make use of my pen and napkin while Seth continued his five star presentation.

Nearing the end of his speech, I could tell Seth held the audience in the palm of his hand. They loved him, loved the vision he'd painted, and were ready to buy into his venture lock, stock, and barrel.

"In summary," Seth said, "our company will provide hope. Hope for people who currently live with and die of incurable diseases. Hope for other researchers and ventures with the potential to change the world but not the funds. Hope for a future of medical research that is built on integrity. Hope for tomorrow. With this in mind, Dr. Hawkins and I thought our foundation was too vibrant to be saddled with a boring name like the Hawkins McAllister Research Foundation. Tonight, we would very much like to introduce and officially open the Tomorrow Foundation!"

I felt my mouth drop open in shock. *The Tomorrow Foundation!* I hadn't told anyone, not even Seth, all of the details of my visit to the future. I hadn't been sure how healthy it would be for others to know future events. I had glossed over what I had felt was minor details and stuck with the basic main events. I certainly had never mentioned the role or even the name of the Tomorrow Foundation!

Suddenly it seemed that a lot of puzzle pieces clicked into place, and the end result was a lot smaller, more interwoven puzzle than I had realized. The Tomorrow Foundation would put Karis, my mother, through school and fund the research that would enable me to survive as a baby and travel back in time.

I felt tears sting my eyes as I remembered everything—when I saved the lives of my grandparents, when I saved Wayne from the drug scandal that would've prevented him from becoming a doctor, when Seth and I saved my Mom from dying in childbirth with Abby, when I went into the future to convince my parents to send their baby back in time, and, now, when the Tomorrow Foundation opened. Everything had one purpose in mind—me. Saving my grandparents enabled Karis, my mother, to be born. Saving Wayne allowed him to develop the medication to save my life. Saving Mom gave me the mother I had always wanted and forced me to question my own origins. Going into the future saved my life in more ways than one and gave me the knowledge I needed to save Seth's. Now, the Tomorrow Foundation would eventually provide the support that would enable all of those events to take place.

Maybe I'd actually been right in my theory after the first time I time traveled. Every piece of the puzzle seemed too deliberate to be random. What value I must have to God who orchestrated everything to make the impossible a reality.

As all of this was downloaded in my brain, I felt humbled and overwhelmed, yet I also felt a great responsibility. It had all been for me. There seemed a purpose behind everything to save my life and make me who I was today. I also realized I had been allowed to change the timeline more than once to save Seth's life and ensure that he was a part of mine. There was a purpose to Seth's life as well, and a purpose in our relationship together. I could never take for granted that I had been blessed with my life and Seth's love in a way and a time that should never have been.

People were leaving their seats and heading toward the dance floor. I listened robotically as Seth, almost as an afterthought, mentioned that, yes, he would be singing. The wonderful band had agreed to humor him, and he had the honor of headlining the first song of the night.

"Are you okay, Hannah?" I looked up to find Wayne beside me again, looking very concerned.

"I'm fine," I assured, trying to stuff my emotions and thoughts back in the closet where I could sort through them later. I took deep breaths and tried to dry my swimming eyes. I couldn't lose the fragile grip I held on my emotions. I hadn't worn waterproof mascara!

"I'm so sorry, Hannah," Wayne moaned, still looking concerned and very contrite. "We never would have done it if we knew it would upset you.

I stared at him a few seconds before realizing what he was talking about. "Oh, Wayne, I'm not upset about what you guys did at all. I kinda wish I was, but I'm not. Unfortunately, I saw the humor. I just realized some things about my trip to the future and my time traveling in general. I was trying to process everything and feeling overwhelmed."

Wayne looked relieved and his eyes brightened. He was always interested in anything I was willing to tell him about my trips, especially the trips to the future. "What did you realize?"

"It's too complicated to explain right now. I'll have to tell you and Seth about it later. But don't think you're getting off the hook that easily. Why did you tell Seth about my plan?"

"Come on," Wayne said, holding out his hand for mine. "Seth is getting ready to perform. I'll explain myself, but

I'm still claiming the dance you promised me."

Despite my protest that the offer was null and void since he already reneged on the agreement, Wayne led me out to the very center of the floor. Before I knew what was happening, Seth's rich voice was weaving a melody, and I was dancing in Wayne's arms.

"Seth's my best friend," Wayne said, shrugging. "Loyalty to him has got to come first no matter what else might come up. I had to tell him. Besides, I thought his idea of turning the tables on you was a lot more fun."

I made a face. "Well, I guess I know now who not to trust."

I thought I saw a brief look of pain cross his face, but he quickly recovered and said with determination. "As much as I hate to hear you put it that way, my loyalty has to always lie with Seth, no matter what I feel."

"I understand that on some level, but it sure would have been nice to give him a taste of his own medicine."

"I gave up on that one a long time ago," Wayne admitted with a smile. "I really don't think it would've worked anyway, even if I hadn't told him. Seth is almost gifted when it comes to sniffing out evil plots against him. It's like he feels a disturbance in the force or something."

Taking Wayne's words as somewhat of a challenge, my brain started working at trying to develop a new plan for getting back at Seth. I certainly wasn't ready to give up. Suddenly, I saw a flash of red and very rudely craned my neck out of the dance for a closer look.

It was Katherine. She was smiling and shaking hands

with people like this was her party. As she turned in our direction, I got a full view of her face and felt a sudden shock of recognition. It was a younger version of the same face I'd seen in the TV in the future. It was the face of the woman who'd been making announcements as to the effectiveness of new government medical policies.

"What's wrong?" Wayne asked, turning in the direction of my startled gaze.

Fumbling, I answered. "I... um... guess I didn't expect to see Katherine."

Wayne made a face. "Well, I certainly didn't invite her!"

Startled again, I put aside thoughts of my newest revelation and focused on Wayne. "I didn't realize you two were officially 'off-again.'"

"We're not. We're off for good this time."

"If she's not here for you, then why is she here at all?"

"Seth invited her."

Immediate panic and jealousy flared up before I could throw a bucket of reason on it.

Oblivious to my turmoil, Wayne continued, "She came by the facility last week. I hadn't seen or talked to her since we officially broke up right after her Hawaii trip. She didn't want to see me, though. She wanted to talk to Seth."

"Why?" I asked, still feeling threatened. "I didn't think Seth and Katherine had much to do with each other even when she was your girlfriend."

"They didn't. But I guess she heard about the attack and attempted mugging. Katherine's really hard to read. I guess she cared and felt more remnants of her friendship with Seth than any of us realized. She was certainly upset when she came to talk to him. Seth is such a pushover. He talked to her awhile and assured her that he was fine. I didn't hear the conversation, but I gathered that he felt sorry enough for her that he tried to console her by inviting her to the opening tonight."

"I wouldn't think the Tomorrow Foundation would interest her," I said, the flames of jealousy finally simmering down with Wayne's explanation, "but I guess the glamour and guest list would."

"Exactly," Wayne agreed. "And with her new involvement with politics, she is especially interested in wealthy influential voters."

"Is Katherine running for office?"

"She certainly is. She is trying to be one of the youngest state senators to be elected. Look at her, she's already an expert politician."

He was right. Katherine was in her element. You couldn't help but notice the beautiful blond in the red dress. She held a captive audience as she held serious conversations, shook hands, and exuded charm. She seemed so genuine. No one would suspect she wore a façade along with her designer gown.

"And you didn't want to hitch your wagon to her political train?" I asked.

Wayne snorted and answered adamantly. "No. That was actually the last straw in our relationship. I always knew she had some extremely liberal views and very little patience for my beliefs or values. In fact, we have opposing views on about every major political, religious, or moral issue. When she started running for office, I realized I couldn't be with someone I wouldn't even vote for!"

Watching Katherine's performance, I felt a sense of dread and hopelessness. I realized it was possible that Katherine held a much higher position in the future than I really wanted to admit. At the time, I hadn't been able to determine if the woman giving the news conference was just a press secretary or the president. All I knew was that this woman, who pretty much hated me, was currently destined to be in a very powerful position in a very scary future government.

"Sounds like you were pretty smart about it, Wayne," I said, still watching Katherine. "I honestly never thought she was good enough for you. I'm sure it was difficult, but I think you'll be better off without her."

"I know. It's hard to think of how many years I wasted with her. I kind of wish you could have told me not to bother with Katherine when you came back in time and we initially met."

I laughed. "At the time, I didn't know what would happen with you and Katherine, and I certainly didn't know how Katherine would turn out. Besides, it's not like you would have listened to me." Wayne shrugged, and I continued. "But, if I'm ever in that time frame again, I'll put it on my to-do list."

"Well, I appreciate it," Wayne replied, "but I wouldn't want you to go that far. You're being careful to take the Hannahpren at the same time each day, right?"

I rolled my eyes. Wayne had somewhat humorously

dubbed my medication 'Hannahpren.' He also called the medication that had originally used Karis's formula and saved my life, 'Karisenol.' The man almost seemed prouder of the names than of the actual medicine!

"Yes, Dr. Hawkins," I replied, "I am being extremely OCD about it. Time traveling is definitely one experience I'd never like to repeat."

"Hopefully, you won't ever have to. The medication seems to be working well. As long as you're careful about taking it, I think you can relax. You've got some other goals to work on—other ways to change the future. Speaking of which, how is school? Seth mentioned that you decided to get started early and are already taking a class before the fall semester officially begins."

I made a face. "School is fine. I've never pretended to like Chemistry, so it's no surprise that I still find it extremely boring. I keep telling myself that it won't take very long to finish the graduate program, and then I can better help you and Seth at the Tomorrow Foundation."

Despite the fact that I was starting a graduate program in Chemistry, I still hadn't given up on my Art. In fact, Seth's mom had told me a couple days ago that a friend of hers owned an art gallery here in the city and wanted to see some of my work. As much as I hated the idea of using someone else's influence to further my own goals, I tried to convince myself that my future mother-in-law's offer was just good networking. As much as I hated Chemistry classes, I loved that I would be able to stay close to Seth here in San Francisco, and, in spite of myself, I was excited about the art gallery opportunity.

"I have a couple of friends at the university," Wayne

said. "From what they say, you're pretty impressive. But, then, I already knew that."

"It somehow doesn't comfort me to be 'pretty impressive' at something I really dislike."

"You won't dislike it when you're done with the program. I won't make you do a doctorate program. We'll find your niche and you'll enjoy using what you've learned to help others. But don't worry, Hannah, Chemistry isn't the only thing you're impressive at. Trust me, Seth is a very lucky man."

Wayne started to say something else, but stopped. I made the mistake of looking into his eyes. They held a pain I didn't understand and an emotion I didn't recognize. Was he feeling bad about Katherine again? He didn't have anyone in his life anymore. Searching his eyes, I tried to understand what he was thinking. I suddenly was very conscious of his arms holding me close as we danced.

Nervously, I broke eye contact, focusing instead on movement to my left. Katherine was gliding smoothly toward a group of people, her royal blue dress making her an eye-catching silhouette.

"I thought Katherine was wearing a red dress," I said, momentarily forgetting my discomfort with Wayne in my confusion. "Did she change?"

Turning to look, Wayne laughed. "No, Hannah. Katherine is still wearing red. Look a little closer."

Obediently, I studied the woman in the blue dress. She looked like Katherine. Same blond hair, thin figure, high cheekbones. I suddenly realized she was now standing next to a woman in a red dress—Katherine.

"Does Katherine have a twin?" I asked, thoroughly shocked and confused.

"Not quite. The woman in the blue dress is her younger sister, Anastasia. They look similar enough to be twins, but if you were closer, you could tell them apart. Anastasia is slightly taller and her eyes are different than Katherine's."

"I didn't realize Katherine had a sister," I said, not liking the idea of two Katherines in the world. "Do they act the same as well as look the same?"

"Yes and no. Anastasia is kind of like an intense Katherine. She is intelligent and more driven in her goals, but she is also more naturally social when she wants to be. Katherine can come across as stiff and snobbish whereas Anastasia can seem very down to earth and charming. I've never been able to determine, though, if it's genuine with Anastasia or if she's just a gifted actress. I do know that she would have never been caught in even a hint of a drug scandal like Katherine was."

"She's not the type to be involved with something like drugs?" I asked, a little hopeful that maybe Anastasia had a different set of values than her sister.

"I wouldn't say that. I just know that Anastasia would have never gotten caught."

I was silent. My hope suddenly transformed into fear, and I mentally labeled Anastasia with a 'Beware' sign.

"She's Katherine's campaign manager," Wayne continued. "With her daddy's funds and her sister's smarts, I don't see how Katherine can lose the election."

“Lucky us,” I muttered.

“All right, Wayne,” Seth’s voice interrupted. “Hand over my fiancé. You’ve been monopolizing her enough.”

“What are you talking about?” Wayne said, adopting a look of hurt innocence. “I was just doing you a favor while you were enjoying your adoring fans.”

Seth’s one song had turned into several. Over Wayne’s shoulder, I’d seen doe eyed debutantes walk to the stage and talk to him, I assumed to bat their eyelashes and request him to sing one more song. Some days I wasn’t sure I could handle being married to such a gorgeous man. I was definitely going to have to work on my insecurities.

“I’m going to head over and see if there’s any food left anyway,” Wayne said, releasing me to Seth. “Hannah, you let me know if he bothers you in any way. I’ll take care of him for you.”

“Sure, Wayne,” I said sarcastically, “just like you helped me tonight? I think I’ll ‘take care of him’ myself from now on.”

Seth laughed, but, instead of dancing, he led me off the floor and behind a pillar.

“You’re not mad, are you?” He asked softly, concerned eyes probing mine.

I wanted to laugh. Seth may put up a lot of bravado at times, but he really couldn’t stand the thought of me being hurt or upset at him.

“No,” I replied, “but I want to be. You’re such a… “ Not able to find an appropriate word, I finally finished lamely, "turkey."

Seth nuzzled my ear and whispered. "It was fun! I really do hate public speaking, but it was so worth it! You're more than welcome to try to surprise me any time you want!"

I groaned. "You know, I just might hate you!"

Seth laughed. "You might if you didn't love me so much!"

I couldn't argue with that. He might drive me insane at times, but I adored him. Whisking me back out on the dance floor, I tried to keep up as Seth twirled me around in a version of the swing to a fast paced song.

Seth was a much better dancer than me, although he was quite efficient at dragging me around. The song ended, and I paused to catch my breath. My eyes focused across the room on Katherine's red dress once again. I hadn't seen her dance at all yet. She was still holding a rapt audience under her spell.

"Maybe I should run for office," I announced, spouting the first thing that had popped into my head. Before Seth could respond, I quickly added, "Not now, of course, but maybe sometime in the future. I might be able to change a lot with a career in politics."

Seth turned to face me, slightly incredulous. "Now you want to be a politician? It seems like only yesterday you were talking about being an art gallery owner, a teacher, an art restorer, an office manager, and a researcher for the Tomorrow Foundation." His eyes were dancing as he ticked off each profession on his fingers. "Hannah, I can't keep up!"

Placing my hands on my hips and matching his teasing with my own incredulous look, I countered. "It really isn't that difficult, Seth. I mean, a lot can happen 'only yesterday.'"

Seth paused, then, tipping his head back, he laughed. Pulling me forward, he wrapped his arms around me. "In your case, Hannah, that is very true. A lot can happen yesterday. But, hopefully, now we're done with all of your yesterdays."

Realizing the band had already begun a romantic ballad, Seth pulled me close in a slow dance. Nuzzling my neck, he whispered in my ear. "I do admit that right now, more than your potential political career, I'm more concerned about the future when the woman I love will finally be my wife."

Immediately forgetting about Katherine and all thoughts of a politics, I pretty much melted into the equivalent of a school girl who just got picked to dance with the hottest guy in school. I really couldn't think beyond the scent of Seth's sexy aftershave and his killer smile. It still felt surreal to realize that Seth McAllister loved me.

The best minutes of the entire night were spent dancing in Seth's arms. I relaxed, enjoying the feel of him holding me close as we moved to the music. Savoring a rare moment of pure contentment, I began to lean my head on his shoulder. Catching a strange sight over his shoulder, I paused, my head never reaching its intended resting place.

Katherine was no longer entertaining a group. Instead, she was standing in a corner talking with Abby's husband, Tom. I didn't think they had ever met before, but they seemed friendly enough now to be having a fairly serious conversation. Seeing them together bothered me in some way, but I couldn't really explain it.

The song ended, and Seth released me. The band announced this would be their last song as they would be taking a break for the auction to begin shortly.

"Come on," Seth said. "Let's go outside and get a little fresh air. I won't be needed for the auction. I'm showing some definite symptoms of heat stroke in this penguin suit."

"You go on ahead," I said, somewhat distracted. "I'll be right out."

Seth must have been miserable because he obediently headed for the French doors to the balcony without bothering to question me further.

Scanning the room, I tried to locate Abby. I needed to know that she was okay. Questions and possibilities raced through my head as dancers twirled around the room finishing the last dance before the auction. Why wasn't Abby with Tom? Had they had an argument? I well knew that any woman would have a serious battle with her inferiority complex seeing that her guy held the complete attention of the beautiful Katherine Colson. Was Abby upset and crying somewhere?

To my relief, I finally spotted Abby twirling around and laughing as she danced with Dad. As they finished dancing, they joined Mom, and headed toward the chairs. Abby looked blissfully unaware of her husband's whereabouts.

Sighing, I turned toward the balcony door, making a mental note to, no matter how busy I was, do a little more prying into the status of Tom, Abby, and Silver Springs. I hadn't been able to shake the feeling that something wasn't quite right, and what I'd seen and heard tonight only heightened my suspicions. If my sister was having trouble, I intended to be there to help her through it.

Full length windows lined the side of the room leading to the balcony. With the black backdrop of night, the brilliant lights of the chandeliers and the bold colors of formal attire reflected in the glass. As I neared the door leading outside, the corner of my eye caught a glimpse of movement reflecting in the glass. Startled, I whirled, looking frantically for the source of the reflection. In that brief second, I could have sworn I had recognized the person whose image had fluttered in with the lights and colors in the window. It was the woman from the future. The woman who had escorted me into the research facility and called me by name.

Heart pounding, I scanned everything and everyone in close proximity to me. She was gone. But she couldn't have moved that quickly, my mind objected. Thoroughly confused, I turned back to the window where I'd seen her. There, amidst the lights, I saw a vague shadow. Walking forward slowly, the outline grew more distinct, though the details were still blurred. I knew for certain now that I was looking at the woman I had met in the future.

With a sick feeling in my stomach and a knot in my throat, I raised my right hand. The woman in the window raised her left hand. Our hands matched.

It was me! My memory filled in the missing details of the woman staring back at me. Her skin had sagged slightly more than mine. Fine lines had traced her eyes, mouth, and neck.

But, our features were the same. It was an older version

of my face, but it was definitely my face.

I tried to swallow, but my mouth was too dry. It had been me! I had met myself! As an older version of myself, I had been there to make sure history would go the right way.

It seemed so obvious now, I didn't know why I didn't recognize myself sooner. In my defense, people never expect to meet an almost forty-years-older version of themselves.

I'd never spent much time looking in the mirror and trying to predict what I'd look like near age sixty. I guess it proved that I never have had an accurate view of myself. I remembered she had said something like she'd never realized how beautiful I was. I'd thought she was stunning as well.

The one thing that had troubled me about her appearance, though, had been her eyes. They were so sad, almost grief-stricken. Transfixed, I stared at the window, searching the black depths of my eyes where that sadness might one day reflect.

Straightening my spine and taking a deep breath, I broke the spell and looked once again fully at the woman in the window. With determination, I tackled my fear. That woman I met may have been me then, but she was not the woman I will be now. I had changed the timeline. I'd saved Seth's life. If her sadness was because Seth McAllister died in her timeline, I would not encounter the same grief in this new one. I had fixed it.

I would figure out the exact date I needed to be at Intrepid Research Facility thirty-five years from now. I would meet myself there and pull the strings to get a young

Hannah into the facility. I would give the instructions "Hannah, say yes." But, I would not feel the grief that woman had obviously gone through. Those sad eyes would not be in my future.

Stepping to the door, I quickly opened it, effectively erasing the images in the glass. The woman in my reflection disappeared, and I walked through the door to meet my future husband.

For this one breathtaking moment, everything was perfect, as it should be. I thought I had escaped those haunting, sad eyes. I no longer feared myself and the full range of my emotions. I was now free to enjoy every minute of my today, dream of my tomorrow, and hope my yesterday stayed in the past.

TIMELINE

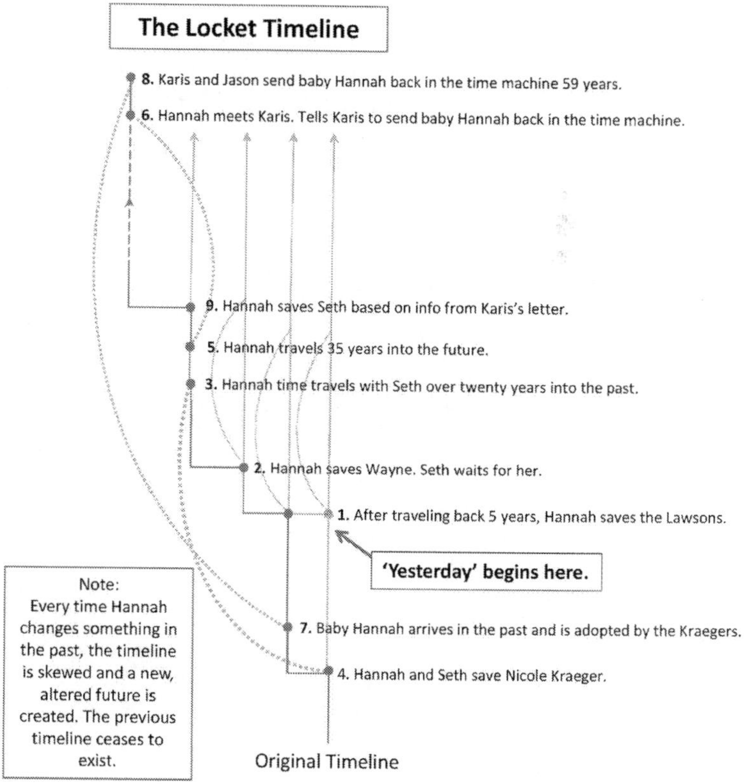

The Locket Timeline

8. Karis and Jason send baby Hannah back in the time machine 59 years.

6. Hannah meets Karis. Tells Karis to send baby Hannah back in the time machine.

9. Hannah saves Seth based on info from Karis's letter.

5. Hannah travels 35 years into the future.

3. Hannah time travels with Seth over twenty years into the past.

2. Hannah saves Wayne. Seth waits for her.

1. After traveling back 5 years, Hannah saves the Lawsons.

'Yesterday' begins here.

7. Baby Hannah arrives in the past and is adopted by the Kraegers.

4. Hannah and Seth save Nicole Kraeger.

Original Timeline

Note:
Every time Hannah changes something in the past, the timeline is skewed and a new, altered future is created. The previous timeline ceases to exist.

WHILE the ***Yesterday*** series is a fantastic story filled with twists and excitement, it is also intended as an extra-ordinary example of the way God works in our lives to accomplish His purpose and mold us into who He wants us to be.

The over-arching theme of ***The Locket*** has to do with Hannah finding out who she is—as a person, as a daughter, and as a child of God. Like the first book, it is a continued illustration of Psalm 139, yet it delves more in depth as to our identity and God's work in our lives.

As you read this book, did you think about the way God works in your own life? As you look through your own yesterdays, can you see God's hand in the events of your life, molding you into the person He has called you to be?

I've always had perhaps an overly simplistic view of

God in that I sometimes picture Him as being a master at jigsaw puzzles. Jigsaw puzzles have to be put together just right—you can't ever replace one piece with another. In that sense, each of our lives is like a jigsaw puzzle with

God being the only one who knows how the individual pieces work together to create the beautiful, finished picture. He puts each piece in exactly the right place in an intricate design, and He makes no mistakes. To us, individual pieces can seem chaotic and pointless when in a pile, but God already knows how all of the events interlock to make us into the people He plans for us to be.

As you answer these questions and reflect on the book, may you see some of the beauty of God's work in your own life. I pray your fellowship and discussion blesses you in your relationship with God as you search the scripture, reflect, share, and pray. May the Lord draw you close to Him and give you the wonderful assurance of His love and purpose in your life.

Finally, may you recognize that what you may see as a pile of random pieces, He already sees as His finished work in all its beauty.

Your eyes saw my substance, being yet unformed. And in Your book they all were written, the days fashioned for me, when as yet there were none of them.

Psalm 139:16

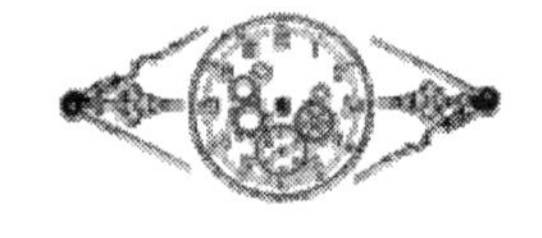

Like most of us, Hannah defines herself by her relationships—a daughter, a sister. But when she discovers she is not who she thought she was, her entire identity is in question.

1. Beneath her roles in life, who do you think Hannah is as a person? What are her character traits? Her strengths and weaknesses?

2. Too often we also define ourselves by our roles in life. But who are you? If you had to describe yourself independent of your relationships, what kind of person are you?

3. Are you the person you want to be? Are you the person God wants you to be?
Ephesians 2:10, 2 Peter 3:10-12a

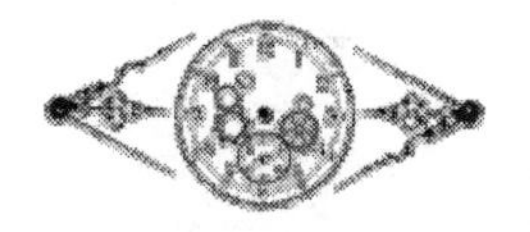

Hannah is given a death sentence. She thinks that it is only a matter of time before she time travels again, and the consequences will kill her.

4. Sometimes in life, things happen that are so difficult and awful that it seems random and without purpose. What in your life has happened that has shaken you to your core? Maybe it hasn't shaken your faith, but what has happened to cause you to come face-to-face with life in its harshness?
Jerimiah 29-11-14, Habakkuk 3:17-13

After waiting for over a month for Seth and Wayne to come up with a "cure" for her problem, Hannah decides to take matters into her own hands. Of course, things don't go according to plan.

5. Do you think Hannah did the right thing to try to seek out her own answers without waiting for results or help from Seth and Wayne?

6. Sometimes in life, we are forced to wait for the answers to our prayers or even for a trial to be over, but waiting can be one of our most difficult assignments.

Tell of a time when you had to wait. Did you get impatient and try to do things on your own, like Hannah? Or maybe you're still waiting and can use some prayer or encouragement.
Psalm 42:9-11, James 5:7-8, Psalm 40:1-8

7. Looking back on your life, can you see instances where patience was rewarded? When the waiting was finally over, was there a reward?
1 Peter 5:6-7

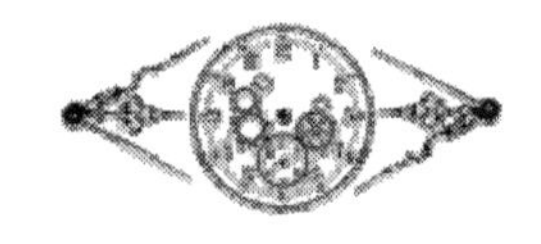

Hannah realizes that the events of her life have been too bizarre and complicated to be random. She feels that God is the one ordering her steps.

8. What examples do you see in the Bible of God arranging events in a seemingly complex way to accomplish His purpose?
Genesis 50:18-20, Matthew 1:1-17

9. What about in your own life? Has God ever taken you on the 'scenic route' to get to a destination? Looking in the rearview mirror, are you now able to see a purpose in the journey? How would you be different you hadn't had those specific experiences?
Genesis 50:18-20

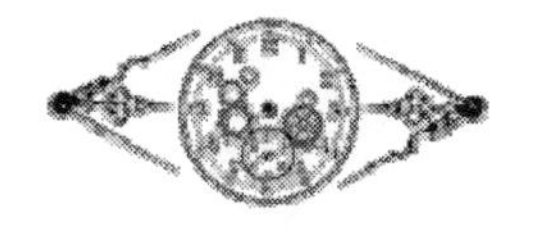

Sometimes our faith for the future is encouraged by looking back to see what God has done in the past. Toward the end of the book, Hannah reflects, "What value I must have to God who orchestrated everything to make the impossible a reality."

10. Are there any examples in the Bible where God did something that should be impossible in order to fulfill His love, purpose, and promise?
Matthew 1:18-23

11. What about your own life? Can you think back, reflect on your path, and see evidence of His guiding hand? Whether miraculous in the traditional sense or not, most people can recount times when they were in the right place at the right time. What events or blessings in your life speak of His love for you? ***Psalm 138:7-8***

If you used this guide as a group discussion, before closing in prayer, please read ***Psalm 139.***

NOTES:

The Yesterday Series:

Book 1: Yesterday

Book 2: The Locket

Book 3: Today

Book 4: The Choice

Book 5: Tomorrow

Book 6: The Promise

FIND all the stories in the ***Yesterday*** series wherever fine books are sold.

The Tru Exceptions Series:

Book 1: Baggage Claim

Book 2: Point of Origin

Book 3: Mirage

Stand-Alone Novels:

Secret Santa

The Romance of the Sugar Plum Fairy

Random Acts of Cupid

The Assumption of Guilt

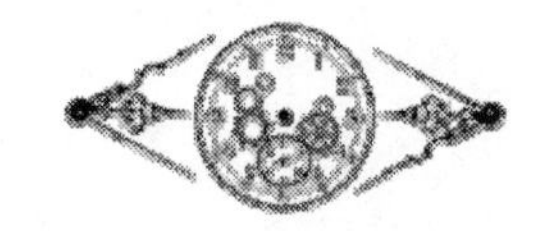

ENJOY this special excerpt from ***Today***, book 3 in the ***Yesterday*** series, available now wherever fine books are sold.

I felt muscular arms around me, and my heart skipped a beat. Waking more fully, I felt the warmth of Seth's bare chest on my skin and the slight whisper of his breath on my cheek.

His eyes were still closed in sleep as his body rose and fell with slow, gentle breaths. Strands of my own long, auburn hair reached across the white pillow to his wavy blond.

In awe of this beautiful creature asleep beside me, I gently caressed a line from his muscular upper arm all the way to his fingers.

He was mine.

Faint gray light crept around the edges of the drawn curtains as I watched Seth sleep and memories of yesterday flooded over me. I was Seth's wife! We had spent so much time anticipating, planning, and preparing. Yet in the end, it had happened so fast that my mind couldn't wrap around the fact that I was now Mrs. Hannah McAllister.

The ceremony had been mid morning, followed by an outdoor luncheon reception. Always expecting the worst case scenario, I still couldn't believe everything had gone so seamlessly. Our families, extended families, and friends had all attended. My sister, Abby, had been my matron of honor, and Seth's best friend, Wayne, had been his best man. My dress fit, the rings didn't get lost, and I managed to repeat my vows without crying or stumbling over the words.

But, best of all, with love in his blue-green eyes and no hesitation, Dr. Seth McAllister had said "I do."

The reception was held at Seth's parent's house in Pacific Grove, and, at their insistence, my new in-laws had spared no expense in the lavish party. The California summer weather was beautiful, making the ocean view breathtaking. I was told that the catered luncheon was delicious and the wedding cake unusually good. I think I ate a few bites, but I was too excited and busy greeting everybody that the taste never registered. Wayne caught the garter, and my bridesmaid, Natalie, caught the bouquet.

Leaving the reception was a bit like trying to navigate no-man's land as showers of rose petals and birdseed bombarded us. Making our escape in a heavily bedecked white Rolls Royce, we drove directly to the airport to catch our flight to Hawaii.

All in all, it was perfect—maybe too perfect. Events in my life have never seemed that easy, and part of me was a tiny bit superstitious that everything really was too good to be true.

Arriving on the island of Kauai before dark, we checked into our room at the resort and didn't leave. We had saved intimacy for our wedding night, and it had been worth it. The wait had made our wedding night more special, more intimate, more passionate. I felt my face heating up with the memories.

The thought of Seth's love for me was overwhelming. I loved Seth so much that, at times, it felt like a physical ache. But that was understandable. Seth was a handsome, highly successful doctor with a line of ladies wishing for any encouragement. I was a lowly wannabe artist who came dragging a long line of strange problems. Seth's gentleness, his fiery kisses, and his words of passion all spoke of a deep love for me that I couldn't seem to understand.

I had never imagined an intimacy that was so exquisite. In Seth's arms I felt cherished, and yet I also felt a passion I never imagined myself capable of. The feel of his warm skin and taut muscles beneath my fingers was something I would never tire of.

Awed by my newfound freedom and unable to resist, I lightly ran my fingers over Seth's back and down his arm again. He stirred but didn't wake.

I wanted to wake him and make sure I hadn't just imagined last night, but I reluctantly decided to let him sleep. The poor man had been putting in long hours helping with wedding preparations as well as tying up research at the Tomorrow Foundation.

On the other hand, I couldn't continue torturing myself by lying so close to a gorgeous man I shouldn't wake.

Carefully, I extracted myself from Seth's arms and crept out of bed. Slipping back on the slinky white negligee that had been decorating the floor, I also grabbed the matching sheer thigh-length robe.

Tiptoeing to the heavy curtains covering the patio doors, I moved one aside and peeked out. The beautiful morning view of the ocean made me catch my breath. Unable to resist, I unlocked the sliding door and quietly slipped out to the private patio.

Although this fourth floor patio was partially enclosed for privacy, I still stayed close to the shadows. My attire wasn't really appropriate for any audience besides Seth. I'd change clothes and come out for a longer time later, but, at the moment, I simply couldn't resist the view.

Though not directly facing East, pink streaks still extended across the sky from a fading sunrise, intermingling with blue and reflecting on the dancing waves past the beach. Breathing deeply, I inhaled the smell of the ocean and the rich, fragrant aroma you can only find on a tropical island.

I was on my honeymoon! My wedding had been beautiful! The man of my dreams—my husband—lay sleeping in my bed!

I couldn't stop smiling. It was a moment I wished I could keep forever. For at that one snapshot of time, I was utterly and supremely happy.

I stood for several minutes, breathing deeply and enjoying the intoxicating happiness course through me as I watched the pink streamers in the sky slowly fade to blue. The spell was finally broken as I became chilled from the slight breeze and my lack of apparel. A nice warm bed, fully equipped with a hot husband sounded entirely too tempting.

If Seth "accidentally" woke up, I could always just apologize later.

I quietly slid the sliding glass door open, moved aside the curtains, and slipped into the room. Before I made it three steps, two pairs of eyes looked up at me from the bed. Neither one belonged to Seth. A man and a woman had obviously been enjoying their privacy in what was supposed to be my bed. Both were wearing less clothing than me.

Shock hit me like a jolt of electricity, and I let out a strangled screech.

The woman began shrieking and clutching at the blankets. The man grabbed at the phone beside the bed and started pounding the buttons.

"I'm so sorry!" I said, my body shaking with shock and confusion. "I must have the wrong room!"

I don't think they could hear a word I said over the woman's continuous high-pitched screams. The man was yelling into the receiver, saying there was a crazy intruder in their room and demanding that Security be sent immediately.

Panicking, my only thought was to get out of there fast. I dashed for the door and ran into the hall. I heard the man yelling for me to stop. Turning right, I ran without thought, expecting to be tackled by burly security guards at any second.

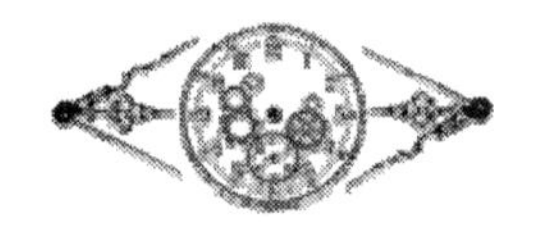

AMANDA TRU loves to write exciting books with plenty of unexpected twists. She figures she loses so much sleep writing the things, it's only fair she makes readers lose sleep with books they can't put down!

Amanda has always loved reading, and writing books has been a lifelong dream. A vivid imagination helps her write captivating stories in a wide variety of genres. Her current book list includes everything from holiday romances, to action-packed suspense, to a Christian time travel / romance series.

Amanda is a former elementary school teacher who now spends her days being mommy to three little boys and her nights furiously writing. Amanda and her family live in a small Idaho town where the number of cows outnumber the number of people.

Connect with Amanda Tru online:
http://amandatru.blogspot.com/

Author site:
http://amandatru.blogspot.com/

Newsletter email sign up:
http://eepurl.com/ZQdw9

Facebook:
https://www.facebook.com/amandatru.author

Twitter:
https://twitter.com/TruAmanda

GooglePlus+:
https://plus.google.com/+AmandaTru

Pinterest:
http://www.pinterest.com/truamanda/

Goodreads:
https://www.goodreads.com/author/show/5374686.Amanda_Tru

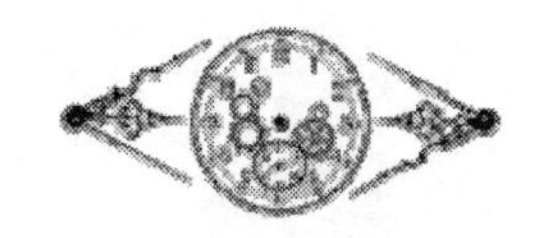

Made in the USA
Lexington, KY
13 August 2016